ONLY CHILDREN

THREE **HILARIOUS**
SHORT STORIES

Books by David Baddiel

ANIMALCOLM

BIRTHDAY BOY

(THE BOY WHO GOT) ACCIDENTALLY FAMOUS

FUTURE FRIEND

HEAD KID

THE PARENT AGENCY

THE PERSON CONTROLLER

THE TAYLOR TURBOCHASER

VIRTUALLY CHRISTMAS

ONLY CHILDREN

ONLY CHILDREN

THREE **HILARIOUS** SHORT STORIES

DAVID BADDIEL

Illustrated by Jim Field
and Steven Lenton

HARPERCOLLINS
CHILDREN'S BOOKS

First published as a collection in the United Kingdom by
HarperCollins *Children's Books* in 2023
Published in this paperback edition in 2024
The Boy Who Could do What He Liked, originally written
and published for World Book Day, 2016
The Girl Who Had Never Been on a Train, originally
published in ebook by HarperCollins *Children's Books*
exclusively for Virgin Trains Ltd in 2016

HarperCollins *Children's Books* is a division of HarperCollins*Publishers* Ltd
1 London Bridge Street
London SE1 9GF

www.harpercollins.co.uk

HarperCollins*Publishers*
Macken House, 39/40 Mayor Street Upper
Dublin 1, D01 C9W8, Ireland

2

Typeset in ITC Novarese Book 12/22pt
Printed and bound in the UK using 100% renewable electricity at CPI Group (UK) Ltd

For Ann-Janine Murtagh

Contents

THE BOY WHO COULD DO WHAT HE LIKED

Illustrated by Jim Field

PART 1

CHAPTER 1

3.32pm

Alfie Moore had a routine. To be honest, he had a *lot* of routines. He had a waking-up routine, a getting-dressed routine, a cleaning-his-teeth-in-the-morning routine, a breakfast routine, a clearing-up-after-breakfast routine, a getting-his-schoolbag-ready routine, a checking-he-had-everything-before-he-left-the-house routine, a walking-to-and-from-school routine, a having-tea routine, a clearing-up-after-tea routine, a homework routine, a limited-amount-of-TV routine, a bath routine, a cleaning-his-teeth-in-the-evening routine (which, to be fair, was pretty similar to his cleaning-his-teeth-in-the-morning routine), a getting-undressed-and-putting-pyjamas-on routine and a going-to-bed routine.

Alfie was eleven and the routines had all been worked out by his dad, Stephen. Each one was precisely written out, listing all the things he had to do, and the times he had to do them by, on pieces of paper pinned up on different walls of his house. For example, the waking-up and getting-dressed routines were on his bedroom wall, along with the getting-undressed-and-putting-pyjamas-on and going-to-bed routines, only on a different piece of paper (placed very neatly next to the first one).

But Alfie never needed to look at those pieces of paper because he knew all his routines by heart. Plus, he wore two watches, one on each wrist (one digital and one analogue, both given to him by his dad) to make sure he always knew the time. As a result, he was never late for school, always knew what clothes to wear, was never tired from going to bed late and always got all his homework done.

Alfie was perfectly happy. The routines made his life work very, very well; it only *wasn't* operating under a routine when he was asleep, although Alfie didn't really know about that because he never seemed to have any dreams.

Alfie's routines did, of course, involve his dad and his stepmother, Jenny. His parents were there at exactly the right times to prepare his tea, to help him with his homework, to kiss him on the top of his head when the back of his head hit the pillow, as it always did at 8.35pm on weekdays and 9.35pm on weekends. But every so often Alfie's parents did go out, to dinner parties and other things that they said they liked, but often came back from crosser and more miserable than they were before they went out. That could mean a disruption to Alfie's evening routines.

Luckily, they had a babysitter who was completely up to speed with how Alfie lived his life. Her name was Stasia and she was Lithuanian. If anything, she was even more efficient than Alfie's dad at making sure Alfie stuck to his regular timetable.

Stasia would arrive, promptly, at 6pm and everything would run smoother than smooth with Alfie's having-tea routine, his clearing-up-after-tea routine, his homework routine, his limited-amount-of-TV routine, his bath routine, his pretty-similar-to-the-cleaning-his-teeth-in-the-morning-cleaning-his-teeth-in-the-evening routine, his getting-undressed-and-putting-pyjamas-on routine and his going-to-bed routine.

But then, one day, Alfie came back from school to find his stepmum, Jenny, video-calling Stasia on her phone. He wanted to interrupt her and tell her all about his science class, which he had really liked that day because they'd been doing space travel, but he could see that she was preoccupied.

"But what are we going to do?" his stepmum was saying. "We've got a dinner party tonight. It's Stephen's boss. I really don't think we can cancel."

Alfie's stepmum, it should be said, was not quite as concerned about the routines as Alfie's dad. In fact, if anything, she was a bit worried that Alfie was being teased at school for his punctuality and his always-having-his-homework-doneness: she thought she'd heard a boy called Freddie Barnes shout: "BORING, BORING ALFIE!" at him in the playground.

But she knew the routines had started soon after Alfie's biological mum had died and that they had made day-to-day life much easier while Stephen was a single dad. And, even though Stephen wasn't a single dad any more, he seemed to want to stick with the routines and Jenny didn't like challenging him about how he had decided to bring up his son.

"I am sorry, Mrs Moore," said Stasia from the phone screen. "I cannot help it. My family needs me. I must catch a plane at 7.30."

Jenny shook her head. "How heavy *is* this pig?"

"Was. The pig is dead."

"Dead? Running into your mother killed the pig?"

"No. Because she broke my mother's leg, the pig has been destroyed." There was a short pause. "Although we will eat her later." There was another short pause. "The pig. Not my mother."

"OK..." said Jenny. "Fine. Of course. I understand. Go. We'll... find someone else."

But when she clicked off and looked up, Alfie could tell she was worried. And *he* was worried too because they'd never had any other babysitters, apart from his grandparents, and both sets lived too far away to reach his house in time.

Who were they going to get to look after him?

CHAPTER 2

5.30pm

The situation got worse when Alfie's dad arrived home and discovered that Stasia had to fly back to Lithuania to deal with her emergency pig-induced crisis. Going to his boss's dinner party was *non-negotiable*, he said. Alfie wasn't sure what non-negotiable meant, but it seemed to suggest that his parents were going to go out whatever happened. He started to think they might just leave him home alone or, worse, take him with them and then he'd have to talk to grown-ups about management consultancy, which is what his dad did, and Alfie had even less idea what that actually meant than non-negotiable.

"There must be someone else we can call," said Jenny. "What about the next-door neighbours?"

"They're away on holiday," replied Alfie's dad.

Alfie, not really liking it when his dad and stepmum got frantic, went over to the other side of the living room where there was a chest of drawers. Inside the top drawer there were lots of bits of paper, including some of the bits of paper that his dad had first drawn up his routines on. Alfie liked to look at these sometimes to see how his routines had changed as he had got older.

"OK," said Jenny. "What about the other side? Mr Nichols…"

"Are you serious? He stands all day at the lights on the High Street, directing traffic with a spoon."

Jenny nodded. "You're right. Bad idea." She sat down, took out her phone and started tapping. "We could call an agency…"

"No, Jenny."

"No?"

"No. I don't want someone we've never met. How could we trust them to be on top of everything?"

"On top of every… what thing?"

Stephen looked at her like she was mad. "The routines, Jenny. Alfie's *routines*."

Alfie's stepmum stopped tapping. She put the phone down and sighed.

"Then I'm out of ideas," she said.

Alfie's dad put his head in his hands. "What are we going to do?" he said, sounding muffled.

"What about this?" suggested Alfie.

He held out a small card that he had found under some of the bits of paper in the chest of drawers. It had gone slightly yellow with age, but you could still make out a picture of flowers on it. In the middle of the flowers were printed the words:

MRS STOKES

BABYSITTER

and a phone number. On the back of the card someone had written, in biro:

in case of emergencies

His dad looked at the card. He turned it over. He seemed, for some reason, shocked by it.

"Um… well, I guess… we could try her." He showed the card to Jenny.

"Do you know her…?" said Jenny, surprised.

"No, I don't think we ever used her, but…" He turned the card over so that Jenny could see the writing on the back.

Jenny squinted at it. "Is that…?"

"Yes."

Jenny thought for a while. "Well then, I guess it must be OK. Although, looking at the state of that card, I think Mrs Stokes might be quite old now."

Jenny was right. When Alfie first saw Mrs Stokes, he didn't think he'd ever seen anyone so ancient. She made his oldest grandparent, Grandpa Bernie, look like a member of a boy band. She had a Zimmer frame, two hearing aids and – although Alfie didn't know how tall she might have been before – seemed to have shrunk with age to the size of a munchkin. And it took her so long to walk up the drive that, by the time she was actually inside the house, Alfie wondered if it was too late for his parents to go out.

How on earth, he thought, *is she going to look after me? And, more importantly, make sure I get through all my routines?*

CHAPTER 3

6pm

The first problem, in fact, was making Mrs Stokes understand what a routine *was*.

"Shoe-bean?" she said loudly to Stephen. "Your son has a bean in his shoe? Baked or haricot?"

"No," said Stephen, sighing. He bent down to her ear, which Alfie could see was very small and poking out of her extremely white hair. She was sitting in the kitchen, drinking a cup of tea that Jenny had made, and into which Mrs Stokes had put a seemingly endless amount of sugar.

"ROO-TINE. I said I'd like Alfie, if possible, to stick to his usual *routine*…"

"Oh dear, dear, dear," said Mrs Stokes, looking with concern at Alfie. "I'm so sorry."

"Pardon me?" said Stephen.

"That's all right, love," said Mrs Stokes. "I'm a bit deaf myself." She pulled Stephen's face down by his ear and shouted into it: "I'M SO SORRY!!"

"*Ow!*" said Stephen, pulling away and rubbing his ear. "What about?"

"Your son having to have a *poo-team*," said Mrs Stokes. "I've never heard of that before in such a young person. So, where are they? How many people normally help him go to the toilet?"

Alfie's dad frowned and whispered to Jenny: "I *really* don't know if we should go out and leave Alfie with her."

"Why are you bothering to whisper?" said Jenny.

Stephen looked at Mrs Stokes, who was happily smiling at him. "Good point," he said in a normal voice. "Maybe I should just call it off after all."

"Well, OK, phone your boss and—"

But, as she was saying this, Stephen's phone rang.

"It's him," he said, looking stressed. "He'll be asking why we're not there already. Pre-dinner drinks started at six…" And he dashed off into the hallway, apologising to his boss in hushed tones. Jenny exchanged a glance with Alfie.

"Mrs Stokes," said Jenny, crouching down. Alfie noticed that the old lady was dressed a little bit like the Queen – all in green, with a necklace of pearls – but as if the Queen had bought her clothes at Oxfam. "Alfie doesn't have *a poo-team*. He has *routines*."

"Oh, I see. Where did you get them from, Topman?"

Now it was Jenny's turn to frown. "Sorry, not quite with you, Mrs Stokes."

"His *new jeans*. I prefer Primark myself." She took a sip from her cup. "Lovely spot of tea. Can I have another?"

Alfie watched all this with increasing horror. He looked at his stepmum, but she was writing something down on her phone. She held it out to Mrs Stokes. It said:

MRS STOKES, WOULD YOU MIND PLEASE SWITCHING YOUR HEARING AIDS ON?

The babysitter seemed to consider this for a while. Eventually, she said: "Well, OK. I don't know why you think that's important seeing as we've been having such a lovely chat. But you're the boss. Hold on a minute."

She reached into her ears with both hands and made a series of tiny adjustments to the bits of plastic inside. Her fingers were stiff and Alfie became concerned that she might get them stuck in there. The whole process probably took about three minutes, but appeared to Alfie to last at least an hour.

Suddenly, there was the most terrible high-pitched squealing.

"WHAT'S THAT NOISE?!" shouted Alfie.

"I DON'T KNOW!" replied Jenny loudly. "IT SOUNDS LIKE MY OLD *JESUS AND MARY CHAIN* RECORDS!"

"IT SEEMS TO BE COMING FROM… HER!!" said Alfie, pointing to Mrs Stokes.

"Sorry, dearies," said the old lady. "If I switch them both on together, they do tend to feedback a bit. Hold on a mo."

At this point, Stephen came back into the room. "WHAT'S THAT AWFUL NOISE?!" he shouted.

"IT'S MRS STOKES'S HEARING AIDS!" yelled Alfie.

"WHAT?"

"MRS STOKES'S HEARING AIDS! THE THINGS SHE PUTS IN HER EARS TO HELP HER HEAR!!"

"I CAN'T HEAR YOU!" Stephen bellowed.

Mrs Stokes herself seemed impervious to the sound, fiddling and fine-tuning inside her ears again.

"DO WE HAVE TO GO TO THE DINNER PARTY?" shouted Jenny.

Stephen made a face, meaning, *Yes, probably – but I'm still not happy with Mrs 2,000 Years Old here*. (Alfie was quite good at reading his dad's expressions.)

Jenny thought for a moment and then passed Stephen the card, the old one with Mrs Stokes's name on it and the words *in case of emergencies*. She raised her eyebrows meaningfully. Alfie watched his dad look at the card for a while and then come to some sort of a decision.

"OK," said Stephen. "Fine." He turned towards the old lady. "MRS STOKES! MRS STOKES! WE'RE GOING OUT NOW!!!"

Mrs Stokes nodded and smiled, oblivious to the fact that the feedback from her hearing aids seemed, if anything, to be getting both louder and higher pitched.

"SO, I'D LIKE ALFIE TO STICK TO HIS USUAL ROUTINE IF POSSIBLE. AND DEFINITELY IN BED BY…"

The feedback suddenly stopped. Which meant that when Stephen finished his sentence by saying,

"...9.35PM!!!",

it was much too loud.

Mrs Stokes sat back in her chair and said: "Blimey. No need to shout, dear!"

Stephen shut his eyes and took a deep breath. "I was saying," he said, "that I'd like Alfie to be in bed by 9.35pm if possible. And, before that, to stick to his usual routines."

"Oh. That's no problem," said Mrs Stokes. "Hang on, I'll make a note of it."

She opened her handbag, which smelt so much of mothballs that moths from miles around must have flown away, terrified. Nonetheless, Stephen and Jenny and Alfie breathed a sigh of relief as they watched her write.

"His… usual… blue cream," she said, holding up her pad and reading out the words, which were written in neat, if shaky, capitals. "What is it, a kind of pudding? I like Spotted Dick myself."

CHAPTER 4

6.15pm

Eventually, though, Alfie's parents managed to make Mrs Stokes understand what a routine was. Which meant that Stephen and Jenny could finally leave the house.

They were just about to go out of the front door when his dad paused for a moment by a picture in the hallway.

It was a painting that had been done by Alfie's mum – his real mum – of the sea. It wasn't one of those nice but boring ones, like people sell at craft fairs, of some cottages by the coast. His dad had told Alfie – who was too little to remember – that one of the things his mum had always wanted to do before she died was swim with dolphins. She never got to do that so instead she had painted this amazing picture, swirling with colour and movement and adventure, of what the sea might look like if you were rushing through it underwater.

Alfie had seen it so often he now forgot it was there. But, just at this moment, his dad was staring at it, like the painting had put him into a trance.

"Dad," said Alfie, shaking his father out of it. "Are you sure about… going out tonight?"

Unexpectedly, he heard a voice from the small toilet beneath the stairs.

"Don't worry! It'll be fine! I'll make sure everything's all right here, you'll see!" Mrs Stokes opened the door a little and peeked out at Stephen and Jenny. "You go! You *need* to go! You definitely *need* to go!"

And she shut the door again.

Jenny and Stephen exchanged glances. Stephen crouched down and put his hand on Alfie's shoulder. "To be honest, Alfie, I'm *not* entirely sure. But here's the thing: if you just stick to your routines, everything will be fine."

Alfie looked into his dad's eyes, to see if he was telling the truth. Which was quite hard as they kept on looking off to the side, towards the painting, again.

"What do you think, Jenny?" said Alfie.

Jenny opened her mouth to answer – possibly even to disagree with Stephen a little, from the expression on her face – but Alfie's dad said: "Alfie. Let's not discuss it now. We *really* have to get going. And besides – especially if you're going to be asleep by 9.35pm! – you need to be getting on with your having-tea routine. You're already…" he checked his watch, "seven minutes and forty-three seconds late laying the table."

Alfie checked his watches. His dad was right. He nodded and turned back slowly towards the kitchen.

"Seven minutes and forty-*five* seconds!" said his dad from behind him.

"Oh, come on, Stephen," said Jenny. "We're already late ourselves now!!"

"Oh no!" said Stephen, running out of the door.

CHAPTER 5

6.35pm

Alfie decided to make the best of it. He went and sat at the table, with his plate and knife and fork and glass of water all ready.

The trouble was that Mrs Stokes – who, according to the having-tea routine, was meant to get Alfie's meal out of the oven for him – wasn't with him. She was still in the toilet. She'd been there, Alfie realised, for quite an alarming length of time. He would have been more concerned were it not for the number of strange groaning noises she was making. He'd rather not have heard those sounds, but at least they convinced him that she wasn't – well – dead.

Finally, he heard a flush, followed about two minutes later by the sight of his babysitter humping her Zimmer frame down the hall.

"Mrs Stokes!" said Alfie. "It's Broccoli Bake for tea today! Jenny will have left it in the oven, so maybe, if I help you with your walking frame, you can—"

But Mrs Stokes just carried on towards the living room. Alfie sat there for a bit, not knowing what to do. He was shaken out of his reverie by the sight of a boy on a bike flashing past the kitchen window: a very familiar boy on a very familiar bike.

Oh no, thought Alfie.

"HEY!" shouted Freddie Barnes (for it was he), turning round and cycling back in front of the window. "IT'S ALFIE! BORING, BORING ALFIE!!"

Yes, Freddie Barnes *did* sometimes shout that at Alfie, just as Jenny had feared.

After a little while saying the words "Boring, Boring Alfie" over and over again whilst laughing and pointing – which must have got dull fairly quickly, seeing as he was on his own with no other bullies to share this with – Freddie cycled off.

Alfie shook his head, got down from the table and went through into the living room where Mrs Stokes was sitting in an armchair, watching *Strictly Come Dancing* on TV. She looked completely engrossed.

"Er… Mrs Stokes?" said Alfie. "It's time for my tea. Well, actually…" he added, checking his watches, "… we're already a bit over. We should have been plated up eleven minutes ago. But anyway… you're meant to… bring me my tea."

"Yes, dear," said Mrs Stokes, without moving her eyes from the TV. "Just do what you like."

Alfie frowned. "Pardon?"

"I said, just do what you like."

Alfie wasn't sure how to take this. "But… you're meant to bring me my tea. Then, in the next fifteen minutes, I'm supposed to eat it. Then I clear up, bring my plate and cutlery and glass over to the sink and help you load the dishwasher. That's scheduled to take between six and nine minutes, depending on the size of the meal. Broccoli Bake should be at the lower end of that, I think, which is good because we're already running late."

"Yes, dear," said Mrs Stokes. "Absolutely. Just do what you like." And she turned the volume up on the TV.

Alfie didn't know what to do. So he ran round the house – back into the kitchen, upstairs to his bedroom, stopping on the landing to go into the bathroom, and then back down into the living room. He collected all the bits of paper from all the various walls and then handed them in a neat pile to Mrs Stokes.

"Mrs Stokes!" he said. "These are my evening routines. My having-tea routine, my clearing-up-after-tea routine, my homework routine, my limited-amount-of-TV routine, my bath routine, my cleaning-my-teeth-in-the-evening routine—"

"Is that very different from your cleaning-your-teeth-in-the-morning routine?" said Mrs Stokes.

"Er... no, they *are* pretty similar" said Alfie, slightly surprised that she'd heard what he'd been saying. "Anyway, there's also my getting-undressed-and-putting-pyjamas-on routine and my going-to-bed routine!"

"That's nice, love," said Mrs Stokes.

"No, but you don't understand," said Alfie desperately. "We're already..." he looked at both wrists, "...fourteen minutes late with having-tea. That means all the other routines will be fourteen minutes behind schedule. Unless we can make up some time, maybe on homework… or I guess I could have a shorter bath… But we need to get started!"

"All right, dear," said Mrs Stokes, handing all the pieces of paper back to Alfie. "You get on with it. *Just do what you like!"*

CHAPTER 6

6.49pm

Alfie remembered what his dad had said: *just stick to your routines*. It was clearly no good trying to get Mrs Stokes involved, so Alfie decided to get on with it on his own. He took all the paper routines and laid them out in front of him at the kitchen table. He didn't, after all, need a grown-up to help him through them, did he?

Well, unfortunately, yes. The first one, for example. The one that he was already fourteen –

no, sixteen now – minutes behind for. Theoretically, he could do having-tea himself. But that meant going very off limits in the way the routines were meant to work. He was supposed to be in place, having laid the table, by 6.30pm. His stepmum, or Stasia, would then bring him tea. For him to bring *himself* tea confused everything. Not least because his tea was in the oven, on quite a hot plate, and he knew he wasn't supposed to get hot stuff out of the oven. That was definitely a grown-up's job.

There was one upside to all this: even though he'd accepted that it was always what he had for tea on a Saturday night, secretly Alfie didn't really like Broccoli Bake. He thought about getting something else, but when he looked in the cupboard most of the tins and packages in there contained stuff that needed cooking. Which he also couldn't do on his own.

And time was ticking by. He really needed to get on to his *next* routine, clearing-up-after-tea.

But this presented both a practical problem and a philosophical one. Could he clear up after tea when he hadn't actually *had* any (that was the philosophical one)? He could clear the table, and bring his plate, glass and cutlery to the sink, but he hadn't used them, so did they need to be cleaned? And anyway he didn't know how to switch the dishwasher on; a grown-up had to do that (this was the practical problem).

Then, after that, there was homework. It was science – a whole essay he was meant to write, about the difference between mammals and marine animals… *tonight*. He needed a grown-up to help him with that too. Next on the list was a limited-amount-of-TV and he couldn't do that either because Mrs Stokes was sitting in front of the telly.

Alfie didn't want to go any further down the schedule because, if he couldn't get the next four tasks done, there was just no point. He simply wouldn't be sticking to his routines. Which was what his dad had told him he had to do.

Alfie felt a rising panic in his throat. He knew, at some level, that his world was falling apart. He'd started to sweat and quite a large part of him wanted to cry, which he hadn't done for ages, not since his mum died. The feeling in his throat got worse and a shout came out that was half a scream. It might have been wordless, but it wasn't. It was two words.

"MRS STOKES!!!!!"

It was a last attempt to get the old lady to come and do her bit to make the routines happen.

"YES, DEAR!!" Her voice came through, crackly as ever, from the living room.

"I DON'T KNOW WHAT TO DO!" shouted Alfie.

This, undoubtedly, was playing into Mrs Stokes's hands. "OH WELL!" she shouted, *"JUST DO WHAT YOU LIKE!!"*

Just do what you like? thought Alfie. *Are you going to say that over and over again? Just do what you like just do what you like just do what you like just do what you like!!!!*

"ALL RIGHT THEN!" Alfie shouted, thinking of time ticking away and his routines slipping past. He held his hands up in exasperation.

"I'LL JUST DO WHAT I LIKE!!"

And suddenly he noticed — because his hands were up in the air — that both his watches had stopped.

END OF PART 1

Interlude

"As I'm sure you know, there's a lot of *talk* in our business about doing things *differently* – what people call *out of the box ideas*. But really, with management consultancy, it's all about sticking to what you *know*. Frankly, there is a box, and we've got to put the right things into it before we start thinking about everything *outside* of the box that might be… that might be…"

"Also put into the box?"

"Yes. Thank you, Juliana. We have to know what's *meant* to be in the box before we put stuff from *outside* the box into the box that's not *supposed* to be in there."

Stephen's boss, Trevor McNade – we could just call him Trevor, but he was one of those people who always seemed to demand a surname too – had been talking like this, about *boxes* and *ideas*, while emphasising certain words seemingly at random, for a while. Stephen and Jenny were in a circle of people standing round him, in his very grand living room, under his very grand chandelier. Everyone was holding champagne glasses and nodding. *Really* nodding.

Suddenly, though, Jenny stopped nodding.

"Sorry, Trevor…" – she wanted to say Trevor McNade, but she managed, just, to keep it to Trevor – "…but surely the whole point of thinking *outside* the box is that the stuff you think of – that's outside the box – well, it never goes in the box."

There was a short silence, during which Trevor McNade adjusted his tie, fiddled with his glasses and his suit buttons, and frowned at Jenny. The elegant woman next to him – Juliana – whispered, "Stephen Moore's wife, sir," into his ear.

Stephen glared at Jenny. Jenny mouthed, *What*?

"What do you mean…" said Trevor McNade, "…*never goes in the box*?"

"Well, outside the box means… y'know… outside the box. So the expression refers to ideas and thoughts that are so unusual that we basically have to throw the box away."

Jenny laughed nervously as she said this. No one else joined in. Trevor McNade stared at her, like she was mad, for about a minute – but it felt much longer – and then started talking about something else. At which point Stephen made a furious head gesture to Jenny to meet him in Trevor McNade's very grand hallway.

*

"What?" said Jenny, out loud this time.

"Come on, darling. You know why we're here," said Stephen, looking over her shoulder at the dining room, where guests were starting to sit down for dinner.

"To agree with everything Trevor McNade says?"

"Yes. Basically."

Jenny sighed. "OK. I'm sorry. Let's get it over with. Do you want to call the babysitter and check everything's all right before we begin dinner?"

Stephen nodded and took out his phone. Then suddenly, down Trevor McNade's long and (obviously) very grand staircase, came a young boy wearing a suit and tie and glasses – a suit and tie and glasses very similar to, but a little smaller than, Trevor McNade's.

"Would you *please* get out of my *way*?" said the boy.

"Sorry," said Stephen, moving aside.

"Ridiculous, you *people* cluttering up the *hallway*. My father *specifically* asked me to join his guests in the dining room at 6.49pm as we *sit down* to eat."

"Sorry," said Stephen again.

"Well, just remember that my starter isn't getting any warmer."

"Sorry," said Jenny.

The boy sniffed, as if to say, *Don't do it again*, and moved through to the main room to join the dinner party. Jenny and Stephen heard the words: "Ah! Cyril!" and "How good of you to join us!" and "One minute late though, aren't you?" from inside.

"Cyril seems nice," said Jenny.

"No, he doesn't," said Stephen.

"I was being sarcastic."

"Oh."

"What he really seems like…" said Jenny after a short pause, looking meaningfully at Stephen, "…is a boy whose father has taught him that there is only one way to think: *his* way."

Stephen stared at her, then he turned his attention to the dining room where the guests were all seated. Cyril and Trevor McNade were sitting together, smiling smugly as everyone told them how marvellous they both were.

Stephen put his phone away. "Shall we get out of here?" he said to his wife.

PART 2

Time Stop
6.49pm

That's odd, thought Alfie, looking at his watches both showing the time as 6.49pm. It should have frightened him, but actually it calmed him down. Alfie was so convinced that his watches worked, and couldn't possibly both fail at the same time, that the more likely explanation was that time had stopped. In some way. Which was good news just at the moment, as it meant that he was no longer getting further and further out of step with his routines.

It occurred to him, in fact – as he had frozen in place with his arms still raised – that if time had stopped he might be stuck, unable to move, which could get very uncomfortable. But, actually, he unfroze his arms and got down from the kitchen table easily.

He wasn't quite sure how best to handle the current situation. But he knew that whatever weirdness was going on was something to do with him saying that he would do exactly what he liked. Not just saying it: shouting it.

And he knew that when he'd said it he'd meant it. In a different way to the way in which Mrs Stokes had been saying it. She had meant: *Yes, dear, you just do whatever. I want to watch* TV. But Alfie, in his anger and frustration, had meant: OK, I *will do what* I *like –* EXACTLY *what* I *like – just watch me!*

But, when he had shouted it, what he had liked the idea of – what, in other words, he had wanted to happen – was indeed for time to stop.

And that's what *had* happened.

So maybe... maybe...

Having-Tea
6.49pm

Alfie sat at the kitchen table again, picked up his knife and fork and said again, loudly: "I'll JUST DO WHAT I LIKE!!"

Since they had just stopped time, he assumed these were magic words. So he expected, on saying them, something magical to happen. But perhaps disappointingly – even though a minute before this was exactly what he had wanted – Mrs Stokes appeared in front of him.

"Oh," he said. "Hello."

"So…" she said. "What would that be?"

"I beg your pardon?" said Alfie.

"What would that be? In this particular case."

"Eh?"

"Oh, come on, Alfie, don't be dense. What – seated as you are at the kitchen table, with your knife, fork and plate at the ready – would you *like* to do?"

Alfie frowned. Not just because he was thinking about answering the question – although he was – but also because he had noticed something about Mrs Stokes. She had come into the room very quickly and was standing up straighter than she had before.

She was speaking to him in a loud, uncrackly voice, without seeming to hear any of *his* words wrong and without her hearing aids feeding back. And her Zimmer frame – if Alfie wasn't mistaken – was *lighting up*. In colour! It was like it had been secretly put together from a batch of different coloured lightsabers – red and blue and yellow and green – and she'd only now switched them on.

"Um…" he said, "I'd *like* to eat some candyfloss."

"OK. Just usual candyfloss or…?"

"I'd like it in the shape of a rocket!"

"Excellent! Now you're getting into the spirit of things! Anything to go with that?"

"Er… chips?"

"Rocket candyfloss and chips!"

Mrs Stokes seemed to concentrate. The colours of her Zimmer frame started flashing. And suddenly there it was, in front of him on the table: a tube of the pinkest, fluffiest candyfloss, shaped exactly like Apollo 13, the rocket ship that Alfie most liked from when they had done the history of the moon landings at school.

The chips were built up next to it, a huge side ladder of them, criss-crossing all the way to the top. It was incredible. Although one weird thing was that beneath the candyfloss rocket there was some mash.

"Er…" said Alfie, prodding at it with his fork, "aren't the chips enough potato?"

"That's smoke!" said Mrs Stokes. "From the lift-off!"

"Brilliant!" said Alfie.

"Anything to drink?" she added. "Perhaps something that could help power the rocket…?"

"I don't really want to drink oil…"

"No, but it could look a bit like oil…"

Alfie had a thought. "Well, I've always wondered why no one makes a fizzy chocolate drink."

Mrs Stokes clicked her fingers and a glass appeared next to his plate full of something brown, creamy and sparkling.

"Enjoy," she said.

Clearing-Up-After-Tea
6.49pm

The strange thing about that tea – which might seem, in dietary terms, a little sugary and heavy – is that actually it wasn't. Every bit of the candyfloss rocket that entered Alfie's mouth seemed to change its level of sweetness so that it never became overpowering, the fizzy chocolate went down like a smooth treat and the chips were really light, fluffy and not too greasy.

"It's all organic," said Mrs Stokes, which seemed

unlikely in the case of candyfloss, chips and fizzy chocolate, but then again it was *magic* candyfloss, chips and fizzy chocolate, thought Alfie, so there might be a special exemption.

When he'd finished his tea, she said: "What's next?"

"What do you mean?"

"What routine's next?"

"Oh," said Alfie. "Clearing-up-after-tea."

"OK," said Mrs Stokes, "if you were to go about that just as you liked, how would you do it?"

Alfie thought. His first instinct was to say that he wouldn't do it at all, but he felt that would be rude or possibly ungrateful. So he said: "Plates are a bit like flying saucers, aren't they?"

"They are," said Mrs Stokes.

"How do flying saucers fly, Mrs Stokes? They're round and all their jets seem to be underneath, so how do they fly anywhere but upwards?"

"Well," said Mrs Stokes, her face lit by the flashing Zimmer frame, "they *may* have a propulsion system that creates an anti-gravity effect which curves the jet streams in infinite directions. Or it may just be…" she added, as Alfie's plate floated into the air, "…magic."

The plate hovered in front of Alfie's face, glowing. Then it twirled round.

"Uh-oh…" said Mrs Stokes.

"What?" said Alfie. Mrs Stokes nodded towards the table. The salt-and-pepper shakers were trembling – then they blasted off up towards the plate! Followed closely by a bottle of tomato ketchup, which had also suddenly risen into the air like an enemy rocket ship!

"THE DARK FORCES OF THE CONDIMENT ARE COMING!!" shouted Mrs Stokes.

Alfie picked up his knife and fork and held them

up vertically, like a comic-book picture of a boy expecting food. He levered the knife forward and the fork backwards.

"Go Warp Factor 1! Hyperspeed!!"

The plate zoomed away from his face. Alfie manipulated his knife and fork backwards, forwards and sideways, making the plate zigzag its way through the attacking salt-and-pepper shakers, and enemy-rocket-ship ketchup. Expertly, he controlled the path of the plate up towards the lampshade, along the dining-room wall and past the canvas photo of him when he was a baby that he wished his parents would take down. (It did occur to him that he could

crash the plate into that and destroy it, but he felt that was going too far with doing just what he liked.)

But the shakers and the ketchup speeded up. The condiments were right behind!

"ALFIE!" shouted Mrs Stokes. THE PLATE'S NOT GOING TO MAKE IT! IT'S GOING TO GET SALT-AND-PEPPERED! AND... KETCHUP'D!!!"

Alfie knew what to do. He threw his knife and fork together towards the plate. They whirled round at high speed, like wheels in the air, overtaking the salt-and-pepper shakers, and arcing past the ketchup bottle. Still rotating incredibly fast, they spun themselves on to the side of the plate, giving it that little bit of extra speed it needed... to get to the dishwasher!

Which Mrs Stokes opened just in time for the plate, knife and fork to separate and drop into the right parts of the rack.

"Fabulous," she said. "What about your glass?"

"I think I'm OK just to bring that over," said Alfie.

Homework
6.49pm

Alfie looked at the book he was meant to read. It was big, heavy and called *Marine Biology: An Introduction*.

"Can we just make this one disappear?" said Alfie.

"Yes, why not?" said Mrs Stokes, picking it up. "You'll probably find out what you need to know about this somewhere or other anyway."

With that, she put the book down and walked through to the living room.

"Hang on!" said Alfie, following her. "Isn't the book actually going to disappear?"

"Well, it has, hasn't it?" said Mrs Stokes, looking around. "I can't see it. Now what?" she added, looking down at a copy of the routines she was holding. "Ah! My favourite!"

She picked up the remote control and switched on the TV.

Limited-Amount-of-TV
6.49pm

*T*he *Simpsons* was on. It was a funny episode – the one in which Grampa Simpson turns out to have been a professional wrestler – but after all the excitement involved in having and clearing up tea in the way Alfie had just done, just sitting there and watching TV felt a little… well, for want of a better word… *routine*.

"So," said Mrs Stokes, "are you doing *just what you like*?"

"Well, yes…" said Alfie. "But now it feels like I want *more*."

"Ah," said the old lady. "That's what happens, you see, Alfie, when we get just what we like. Appetite grows. It spirals. The more you're allowed to do exactly what you want, the more you *need* – to satisfy the need *inside*."

"Oh, I see," said Alfie, nodding. "So… this whole experience is, like, teaching me that? About always wanting more and more stuff? Will the next magic thing that happens get out of control and I'll nearly die, but at least I'll have learnt an important life lesson?"

"Nah," said Mrs Stokes.

"Oh, OK," said Alfie. "In that case, I'd like to go into the TV."

And the next thing he knew he was. A yellow, three-fingered version of himself was at the side of the wrestling ring, shouting at Grampa Simpson. Then the channel changed – because Alfie wanted it to, and also because Mrs Stokes had provided him with a remote control to take into the TV. Alfie was now on Cartoon Network in an episode of his favourite show, *The Amazing World of Gumball*. He was a kind of half-frog, half-apple jumping around at Elmore Junior High School.

Unlike *The Simpsons*, this wasn't an episode that had actually been on TV; it just followed a story that Alfie made up as he went along, where Gumball and Darwin were in competition to be his best friend (it ended up with them fighting each other with jelly-and-custard guns and Alfie deciding it was a draw).

Then Alfie pressed another button on his remote control. Some very dramatic music started playing and he found himself in a dark suit and tie, reading the seven o'clock news.

Oh dear, he thought, *wrong button*, as a man poked

his head round from behind a camera, looking very, very confused. *Still, might as well make the most of it.*

"Good evening," said Alfie, "this is the seven o'clock news. All children between the ages of seven and twelve are allowed not to go to school tomorrow. Broccoli Bake has been outlawed. And Freddie Barnes, of 14 Brackenbury Road, is from this moment on to be officially known as Freddie 'Bum-Bum' Barnes. Goodnight!"

And the dramatic theme music started again.

BA-BA-BA BA-BA!

BONG! BO-BO-*BONG!*

BA! BA!

BA-BA!

Bath

6.49pm

Alfie came out of the TV, still wearing the suit and tie.

"You weren't in there very long," said Mrs Stokes.

Alfie shrugged. "It's a limited-amount-of-TV. Always."

"Of course. Why have you kept the suit on?"

"I've got an idea," he said. "For bathtime."

"Ah. Looking forward to it," she replied.

*

When they reached the bathroom – which was on the second floor, and Mrs Stokes seemed to get up there as quickly as Alfie, two steps at a time – he said: "I'm thinking the suit and tie could change into… a frogman's outfit!"

"Fabulous!"

"And then the bath…"

"Just dive in, Alfie," she said.

He did. The suit and tie became a scuba-diving suit and he dived down and down into the bath. Deeper and deeper he went, passing schools of fish and lobsters and whales, before meeting a dolphin, which was standing on its tail underwater, like they sometimes do.

"Hi, Alfie," said the dolphin. "I'm Dolph."

"As in Lundgren?" said Alfie.

"How have you heard of *him*?" said Dolph.

"My dad's a big fan of his old films."

"Right. Well, no. Dolph as in dolphin."

"I see," said Alfie. "How come you can hear what I'm saying underwater?"

"Well," said Dolph, "there are a number of things to consider there. Firstly, in normal scuba-diving, you're not allowed to take the breathing apparatus out of your mouth, which means you can't speak at all. Secondly, I'm a talking dolphin. Called Dolph. So, y'know, let's not worry about it."

"OK," said Alfie.

"Who's the old dear?" said Dolph.

Alfie looked round. Mrs Stokes was floating down towards him. Out of the ends of the legs of her Zimmer frame, which was still lit up, he could see bubbles rushing towards the surface of the water, as if jet-propelled.

"Hello!" she said. "I thought I'd join you for this one. Test out the Zimmer's amphibious capability."

"Great," said Alfie. "But I'm not sure about the new trousers."

"They're not trousers," she said, "they're scales. And a tail. I've gone the full mermaid."

"I see," said Alfie, relieved that she hadn't gone the full, *full* mermaid – above her waist she was still wearing her green if-the-Queen-had-shopped-at-Oxfam top and pearls. *And* carrying her handbag.

"Are you two coming?" said Dolph. "I haven't got all day."

So Alfie and Mrs Stokes swam after Dolph along the bath bottom, which wasn't white and enamel and one-metre long, but covered with coral and infinite. They swam through schools of zigzagging clownfish and crawling lobsters and floating turtles; they hovered above the bright pink and blue coral, speckled by reflected sunlight, out of which long and slinky moray eels peered to look at them; they saw, far beneath them, underwater cities with curly, far-reaching spires and underwater caves where lost treasure sparkled in open ancient, moss-covered chests.

And they also – bit of a bonus – found an old
rubber duck bath toy that Alfie thought he'd lost

Then, suddenly, they were attacked by a school of sharks, approaching in a terrifying V-formation!

"Oh no!" said Alfie. "Is *this* the bit where I nearly

die, but learn my lesson?"

"Nah," said Mrs Stokes. She brought her thumbs and forefingers up to her ears and made a couple of small adjustments. The next thing Alfie knew, a huge piercing wail of feedback was powering out of her hearing aids. The sharks' V-formation fell apart, as they retreated as fast as possible, terrified.

"Thanks, Mrs Stokes," said Alfie.

"Yeah, thanks," said Dolph.

"Pardon?" said Mrs Stokes.

Cleaning-His-Teeth-in-the-Evening

6.49pm

"So," said Alfie, toothbrush in hand, after he and Mrs Stokes had towelled themselves dry and let the bathwater out, "I think the key thing with *this* one is making it different, for once, from the morning version."

"Hmm," said Mrs Stokes. "How are we going to do that?"

"Can I help?"

They turned round. Standing there, in front of

the bath, was Dolph.

"Are you OK to be out of the water?" said Alfie.

"Yes. I'm a mammal, not a fish. I don't have gills. I breathe air just like you, only out of my blowhole." Dolph bent his head and puffed towards Alfie, who felt the – slightly fishy – breath on his face. "As long as I keep my skin damp, I'm OK."

"You see," said Mrs Stokes to Alfie, "you've done your marine biology homework after all."

"Yes, thanks, Dolph," said Alfie. "But meanwhile: teeth?"

"Well, what I do is open my enormous mouth, let loads of little plankton swim inside and they feed on my teeth, cleaning them at the same time."

"*Right*…" said Alfie.

"I'm sensing you don't fancy that much, Alfie," said Mrs Stokes.

"Really?" said Dolph. "I love it. They do a great job and it tickles. In a nice way."

"Maybe this is different enough," said Alfie, squeezing the toothpaste on to his brush.

"How do you mean?" said Mrs Stokes.

"Well, in the morning, I never have a talking dolphin in here when I'm cleaning my teeth."

"Good point."

So he started brushing his teeth. Just for good measure, Mrs Stokes and Dolph joined hands – well, hands and fins – and did a dance, an exact copy of one that Mrs Stokes had just watched on *Strictly* – the American Smooth – to the rhythm of his brush strokes. Just to make sure this teeth-clean was *very* different.

Getting-Undressed-and-Putting-Pyjamas-On

6.49pm

"Let's do this one quickly, Mrs Stokes!" said Alfie, as they went into his bedroom.

"No sooner said than done!"

And the next thing Alfie knew, his clothes had disappeared into the wardrobe and his pyjamas were on.

(There was no nakedness in between, in case you were worried.)

Going-to-Bed
6.49pm

Alfie lay in bed, looking up at Mrs Stokes and Dolph.

"It's probably time to go to sleep now, Alfie," said Mrs Stokes.

Alfie checked his two watches.

"It isn't actually. It's still 6.49."

"Well. Firstly, your watches might be wrong... don't make that 'they never are' face, Alfie, they *might* be. Secondly, you've done all your routines and thirdly,

I'm still your babysitter, and the most important job of a babysitter is to make sure you don't exhaust yourself and be too tired to get up the next morning."

"Is that right?" said Dolph. "I'd say the most important job of a babysitter is to make sure the child they're looking after doesn't die."

Mrs Stokes gave him a look that Alfie could tell meant: I *will not be lectured about babysitting by a dolphin, talking or not*. Alfie wasn't sure whether Dolph would be able to pick up that kind of unspoken message, but he looked away and went *clickclickclickclickclickclick* in what seemed like a told-off manner.

"But," said Alfie, "I've just remembered one more routine!"

"Really?" said Mrs Stokes, opening her handbag and getting out all the pieces of paper from the walls.

"Have you had those with you the whole time?"

"Yes," she said, flicking through them one by one.

"Got to make sure you stick to them." She looked up. "But there isn't another routine. Going-to-bed is the last one."

"No, it's not one I normally do. It's not even one that my dad set up for me. It's one that Freddie Barnes told me he does every night, secretly, when he goes to bed…"

Mrs Stokes frowned. "I thought we didn't like Freddie Barnes?"

"Yeah," said Dolph, "I heard he calls you Boring, Boring—"

"Yes, we're all aware of that," said Mrs Stokes.

"Well," said Alfie, "it's more of a game, really that he made up than a routine. But he told me he does do it every night, so I guess it does count as one."

"Right…"

"Well, I always kind of wanted to try it. But I never did."

Mrs Stokes shrugged. "OK. What does Freddie

Barnes's secret, naughty routine involve, Alfie?"

Alfie smiled, turned his whole body round and dived down under the bedclothes.

Down he went, down and down, even further than he'd gone into the bath. The sheets ballooned around him, as he slid into the depths of the bed. He was joined about halfway down by Mrs Stokes and Dolph.

"W*heeee!*" said Mrs Stokes.

"W*heee!*" said Dolph.

Alfie took this to mean that they'd forgotten their differences.

"SO WHAT HAPPENS, ALFIE?" shouted Mrs Stokes.

"YOU HAVE TO GET TO THE BOTTOM OF THE BED, TURN YOUR BODY ROUND AND THEN GET BACK OUT TO THE TOP

BEFORE THE ENEMY CAN GET YOU!"

As he shouted this back at her, the three of them dropped out of the enormous tunnel of cotton on to some concrete. They landed on their feet, except for Dolph, who landed on his tummy. Mrs Stokes looked around. They appeared to be in the darkly lit streets of a seaside town, near the water.

"Where are we, Alfie?" she said.

"Well, I think it's like… the war."

"Yes, I thought it felt familiar. So…" She rubbed her hands with excitement and looked from side to side. "Who's the enemy? Germans? Viet Cong? Al-Qaeda?"

"No…"

"What's that smell?" said Dolph.

Mrs Stokes looked up and sniffed. "Yes. What is that?"

"That's the bit I haven't told you," said Alfie. "That's what makes it fun! That's why it's called…

ESCAPE FROM FARTY HARBOUR!!"

Mrs Stokes and Dolph looked at him.

"Right," she said eventually. "So, if I understand you correctly, Alfie, what you're saying is that you *let one go* just now? Before we all dived into the bed?"

"Yes. That's what Freddie told me you have to do. I kept it in specially until the right moment."

Mrs Stokes and Dolph looked at each other.

"Er…" said Dolph. "You know I was explaining just now about how I breathe air just like you, only through my blowhole?"

"Yes?"

He nodded his head towards the town. A huge green gas cloud was billowing over the rooftops, coming straight towards them.

"I wish I didn't," said Dolph.

As he said this, many people came staggering down the streets, choking and fainting and crying for help.

"OH MY GOD!" shouted Mrs Stokes. "RUN FOR IT!"

"ESCAPE FROM FARTY HARBOUR!" shouted Alfie enthusiastically.

"Yes!" said Mrs Stokes. "Let's very much hope we can!"

"It's been nice knowing you!" said Dolph, and then he dived into the sea.

Mrs Stokes and Alfie ran along the seafront, splashed a little by the water coming off Dolph's escape dive. But it was windy, as it often is by the sea, even by a sea at the bottom of an eleven-year-old boy's bed, and the terrifying green cloud was catching up with them.

"COME ON, MRS STOKES!" shouted Alfie.

"I'M GOING AS FAST AS I CAN! I'M AN OLD WOMAN!"

"BUT YOU'RE A MAGIC OLD WOMAN!"

I'M NOT *THAT* MAGIC!!" she said in between great panting breaths.

She was slowing down and starting to hobble along. In fact, as Alfie stared back at her, he realised she was looking more like she had done when she'd first arrived at his house.

He stopped running and took her hand.

"IT'S NO GOOD, ALFIE!"

"NO, COME ON, YOU'LL BE FINE!"

But, even as he said it, his nose twitched and he realised it was too late: they had been enveloped by the terrible cloud.

"Actually, I don't think it smells that bad…" said Alfie.

"Of course you don't!" said Mrs Stokes. "No one thinks their own ones do! But I… *urrgggghhh*!!!"

She coughed, spluttered and fell to the ground.

"MRS STOKES!" shouted Alfie.

"HOLD YOUR BREATH!"

"I can't, dear," she whispered weakly. "I hardly have any breath at the best of times…"

Her eyes began closing. The green cloud became thicker and smellier. Even Alfie now felt he didn't want to breathe it in. *That's the last time I eat candyfloss rocket and chips*, he thought. *And as for fizzy chocolate…*

"Mrs Stokes! Mrs Stokes! Is *this* the time things get out of control and I nearly die, but learn my lesson?!"

"Nah," said Mrs Stokes.

"Oh good."

"I think it's the time things get out of control and *I* nearly die," she said.

"No, Mrs Stokes! No!"

"It's OK, Alfie," she said. "Well, it's not OK, it's absolutely disgusting. But I mean it's OK to leave me. I'm an old woman."

"But you're a magic old woman!"

"You said that before. And as I said at the time – it was only about two minutes ago so I don't know why I'm having to repeat myself so soon – I'm not *that* magic. And now, I'm afraid, the overwhelming stinkiness of your fart has taken away all that's left… of my magic… Save yourself, Alfie. Save yourself!"

With that, her eyes closed. The green cloud thickened even more around them. Alfie felt the rising panic – the feeling that had first appeared when Mrs Stokes had been saying *just do what you like* over and over again – returning. He wished he hadn't gone off-piste with one of Freddie Barnes's stupid routines. *Of course* that was going to create trouble. He should just have stuck, like his dad had told him, to his *own* routines.

That thought, though, gave him an idea.

The post-school routines were designed to make sure he was in bed at an appropriate time every night, so that he got a good eleven hours' sleep. That was why he had never done ESCAPE FROM FARTY HARBOUR before, even though it sounded like fun. It was part of his bedtime routine to be asleep by 8.35pm on weekdays and 9.35pm on weekends. It was, in some ways, the most *essential* part of all his routines.

And if there was one thing Alfie was good at, it was following his routines. Even tonight with Mrs Stokes, although they'd been very different from normal, he'd still done each routine, one after the other, in the same pattern as usual. Until this last one.

So he said: "Hold on, Mrs Stokes! Hold on!" And raised both his arms, and stared at his watches, and thought hard, as hard as he'd ever thought, about being back in bed, and fast asleep, by 9.35pm (because today was Saturday – obviously – *Strictly* was on). He made the numbers 9, 3 and 5 (with one dot after the 9) bigger than big, painting them inside his brain like a graffiti artist, until there was nothing, not one thing, in Alfie Moore's mind at all except:

9.35pm

...and an image of himself asleep, as normal, with the watches on his wrists showing that time.

PART 3

CHAPTER 7

10.25pm

"That's really strange, isn't it?"

"Yes. Really strange."

"Why would she send a text like that?"

Alfie stirred, opening his eyes just a little. Through the mist of sleep, he could see his parents standing by his bed, whispering. Although not whispering quite quietly enough, as it had woken him up. Or at least, half woken him up.

"Oh sorry, Alfie!" said Jenny. "We just came in

to check on you."

"I'm fine," said Alfie. "What time is it?"

"It's 10.25..." said Stephen.

Alfie sat up in bed. "You're back early."

Stephen and Jenny glanced at each other.

"Yes...well," said Jenny. "We kind of decided... not to stay too long at the dinner party."

"Oh. What did you do instead?"

Stephen and Jenny's glance became a smile.

"We... went for a walk. In the park," Stephen said.

"A walk," said Jenny, looking lovingly at her husband. "And a run. And a tree-climb. And a dance."

"The park? But it's shut..."

"Yes. We climbed over the fence," said Jenny, her smile widening.

"Jenny! Don't tell him tha—"

"Anyway, time to go back to sleep. We shouldn't have woken you up. Not after you did so well getting to bed at 9.35 like we asked."

"Yes, well... I stuck to all my routines. I did, Dad."

"Did you? Oh..." said Stephen. "Well. That's great, Alfie. But me and Jenny were talking on the way back tonight and we thought maybe we should... loosen up a bit with the routines. I mean, it's good to have *some*, but maybe... maybe it's fine not to worry about sticking to them *all* the time."

Alfie thought about this. But not for very long, as he was really sleepy.

"OK," he said, settling back down under the covers. "By the way, I had the most amazing dream tonight."

"Did you?" said Jenny, surprised.

"Really?" said Stephen.

"Yes. It was fantastic. Mrs Stokes was in it!"

"Oh!"

"Yes. I like her. She's a great babysitter..."

Jenny and his dad exchanged glances again, clearly surprised.

"Oh good!" said Jenny.

"Can I have her again soon?"

"Well… yes. I guess. Depends how long Stasia's mum takes to recover from the pig accident…"

"Have you kept her phone number…?"

"Yes," said his dad and took out the yellowing card with the flowers on it. He held it up and stared at it again. Alfie, even through his sleepiness, could make out the words on the back.

"Dad…" said Alfie, "where did we get the number from? Who wrote that on the back of the card?"

His dad and Jenny looked at each other. Jenny seemed a little bit uncertain, but then nodded.

"Your mum, Alfie," his dad said. "It must have been. It's her handwriting. Mrs Stokes must have been her babysitter when *she* was young. It's odd, though. I don't remember her ever suggesting we use her when…"

"When she was alive," said Alfie.

"Yes," said his dad.

"I suppose she must have written it and put it in that drawer for us to find." Alfie paused. He could feel sleep coming. "In case of emergencies."

His dad looked at the card. Then he looked at Alfie. His eyes were a little moist. "I suppose she must."

Alfie yawned and shut his eyes. "Where's Mrs Stokes by the way...?" A scary memory from his dream came back to him of Mrs Stokes collapsing. From fart poisoning.

"Oh," replied Jenny, "she's just leaving. It's a bit difficult for her to come up the stairs, I think."

Oh good, thought Alfie. She's OK. But of course she is. It was just a dream.

"Hang on..." said Stephen. He went out on to the landing and called down. "MRS STOKES! MRS STOKES! I'LL BE THERE IN A MOMENT TO SEE YOU OUT!"

"NO NEED FOR TROUT!" called up Mrs Stokes, her voice crackly again. "I've already eaten!"

Alfie smiled and turned over. Through the cotton of his pillow, he heard the *ting* of a text coming into Jenny's phone.

"Not *another* one from Freddie Barnes's mum!" she said.

"For heaven's sake," came his dad's voice from the landing. "I mean, it's not Alfie's fault that people call her son 'Bum-Bum'. Is it?"

"Well, she says it is. She says... hold on... *Alfie told everyone to say it on the news*. On the news?!!!"

"Must be a misprint. Autocorrect. Or she's just completely gone mad."

That was when Alfie really started to go to sleep. But the smile stayed on his face.

"MRS STOKES!" shouted Alfie's dad again. "Oh, the old dear hasn't heard me. MRS STOKES!"

"YES, DEAR!" Her voice sailed up from downstairs.

"WE'LL JUST COME DOWN AND SEE YOU OUT!"

There was a short pause. Then, not-crackly but loud and clear and coming up the stairs like a rocket, or a rush of air from a dolphin's blowhole, the words:

"JUST DO WHAT YOU LIKE!"

And, with that, Alfie Moore fell fast asleep.

THE GIRL WHO HAD NEVER BEEN ON A TRAIN

Illustrated by Jim Field

CHAPTER 1

LNER Class A3 4472

C hrissie Connolly loved trains. From the first
time she had seen one – on the cover of a copy
of *Thomas the Tank Engine*, when she was four – she
had been obsessed.

Every birthday since then (there had been seven
of them), all her presents had been train-based.
Train books, train pictures, train-centred clothing
and – of course – model trains. She'd even built up,
in her room, a perfect-to-the-last-details re-creation

of a section of the original London-to-Edinburgh route of the legendary train, the *Flying Scotsman* — the section that would have gone past her house, in fact, on the Scottish border between Berwick-upon-Tweed and Burnmouth.

Where other children of her age might spend hours playing *Call of Duty* (only stopping to say to their parents, "Don't worry, it's definitely a

7+ certificate"), Chrissie would devote the same amount of time to sorting tracks and gauges, and rearranging stations and platforms and scenery, before watching contentedly as her model LNER Class A3 4472 (that's the stupidly technical name for the *Flying Scotsman*) would puff (yes, puff – it had a steam-creating mechanism so that actual little clouds would come out of the chimney, one by one) round and round the track.

Almost every night, when she fell asleep, Chrissie would dream about trains – and usually, in her dreams, she was travelling on the old *Flying Scotsman*, its black chimney puffing out steam.

But Chrissie had never been on an actual train. This was at least partly because she had a spinal deformity, which meant she couldn't walk very easily, and never unaided: most of the time she went around in a wheelchair. Trains these days of course are much easier for people in wheelchairs to get on and off than they used to be, but it wasn't really about that anyway. It was more just that it was tiring for her to go far, and the Connollys had a car that was designed around Chrissie for any small journeys she needed to make.

Chrissie had once said to her mum and dad that maybe she'd quite *like* to go on a train, even if they weren't going anywhere in particular, just for the experience – but they'd looked so tired at the idea, and Chrissie was already so grateful for everything they did for her every day, that she just let it go, and never mentioned it again. Which was how a massive train fan had got to the age of eleven without ever going on a train.

Today, however, that was about to change. Today she was finally going on a train. And not just a tiny journey: she was going on the East Coast Main Line – the *Flying Scotsman's* route – all the way to London.

This wasn't because her mum and dad had

suddenly developed lots more energy. In fact, her mum and dad were not coming with her. This was because they were already in London; they were going to meet her at King's Cross Station and take her where she needed to go, which was a hospital. Chrissie had to travel to London for an operation: an operation that, if it worked, would mean she would be able to walk on her own, at least some of the time. Her parents had done the journey first, in order to meet and talk to the doctors. They had been planning to come back and take Chrissie, but then Chrissie's grandpa, Henry, who was looking after her, had offered to bring her down.

Even though Grandpa Henry was entirely capable of bringing Chrissie to London, her parents hadn't been sure about this. But Chrissie had. Chrissie loved her grandpa. For lots of reasons: one of them was that he had worked on the railways. He had been a guard at Berwick-upon-Tweed station, and a ticket inspector on the East Coast Main Line. So whenever Chrissie wanted extra information about the railways, to make her model more correct in every detail, Grandpa Henry was the first person she'd turn to. He'd tell her everything about what it used to be like – what the trains looked like, and, of course, what they sounded like.

"You mean the sound of the steam, Grandpa, puffing out of the chimney?" Chrissie had said, once.

"Yes," he had replied. "But also the sound of the wheels on the track. You could always hear that, beneath you, as it moved along. B*iddly-da*, *biddly-da*, *biddly-da*!"

Chrissie loved that. Sometimes, particularly when she found it difficult to get to sleep, which happened quite a lot (as it was hard for her to get comfortable), she would use that rhythm in her head as a kind of lullaby. B*iddly-da*, *biddly-da*, *biddly-da* . . . and it would work; she would drift off to it. Although sometimes she'd wake herself up by throwing in a *PEEP-PEEP!!* whistle, too. Which kind of defeated the object.

So Chrissie thought it was perfect that Grandpa Henry would be taking her down to London. By train. And he was looking forward to it, not having done that journey himself for thirty years.

Eventually, Chrissie's mum and dad agreed, thinking that it might be a fun thing for Chrissie to do, and something to take her mind off any worries that she might have about the operation. Which, to tell the truth, Chrissie *was* quite worried about. Not so much that something would go wrong. But more that nothing would go *right*, either. She'd had a few operations before, and they'd all taken a long time to recover from, and none of them, so far, had resulted in any significant improvement.

This one was meant to be different – that was why she was making such a long journey for it – but, in her heart, Chrissie couldn't quite believe that.

Her mum and dad were right, though. The journey *did* take her mind off the operation. In a way they couldn't possibly have imagined.

CHAPTER 2

Biddly-da, Biddly-da, Biddly-da!

All Chrissie thought about as she and Grandpa Henry waited on the platform at Berwick-upon-Tweed station was that, at long last, she was about to go on a train.

As the train approached, and the announcer listed the stations – "calling at Alnmouth, Morpeth, Newcastle, Durham . . ." – Chrissie looked up at her grandpa from her wheelchair and smiled.

"It's going to be great!" she said.

"I hope so, Chrissie!" he replied.

"No . . ." she said, knowing instantly that he'd misunderstood. "Not the operation. Well. Maybe that'll turn out OK, yes." Although, in truth, she doubted it. "No, I mean the journey. The *train*."

"Oh!" said Grandpa. "Yes." Then he frowned, the lines on his face deepening, and said, again: "I hope so."

Chrissie looked up at him, not sure this time what he meant.

It took a little while to get Chrissie on to the train. She decided not to stay in her wheelchair, which she could have done –

there was a space for it in the carriage – because she wanted to sit in a seat. So Grandpa and a nice lady called Karen, in a red uniform, helped her out of the chair and along the carriage. But then – very excitingly, because it meant they had a bit more room and it was easier for Chrissie to walk down the aisle without bumping into so many people – they were moved up from their standard-class carriage to sit in First Class (without even having to pay more)!

U*pgraded* was the word Karen used, although it didn't seem to be a very official decision.

And then they were off! It was *so* thrilling, looking out of the window as they crossed the Royal Border Bridge over the River Tweed, passing the sea, and, in the distance, Holy Island.

But then, suddenly, it wasn't.

The view out of the window turned into fields, and farmhouses, and sheep, and electricity poles, and pylons. Chrissie looked around the carriage. On the seats to her left, a family of four were all staring into their screens, two of them with headphones on. Further back, a bald man was endlessly blowing his nose with one hand, while looking at a newspaper with the other. He was ignoring Karen, who was offering him tea or coffee. Opposite him, a woman Chrissie assumed was his wife was fast asleep. Chrissie craned her neck and, with some pain, looked further up. Two Japanese businessmen were peering at two very complicated-looking spreadsheets on two very thin and expensive-looking laptops.

She looked up. A long row of LED spotlights in the ceiling led her eye to the next carriage, where the chairs and tables and carpets went on and on, the same as in her carriage, the same as on the train that she could now see at the window passing in the opposite direction.

Chrissie shut her eyes. She could still see the dots from the spotlights fading against the inside of her eyelids. She couldn't understand it. She'd spent her whole life thinking about trains, playing with model trains, imagining trains – and now she was finally on one – and she was a bit . . . bored. She felt bad about feeling this way – like she must be spoiled, or stupid, or something – but there was no getting away from the fact that it was true.

"You OK?" said Grandpa, looking over from the other side of the table.

"Yes . . ." said Chrissie.

Grandpa looked at her quizzically. "Chrissie?"

"Yes?"

"Who am I?"

"What?"

"Who am I?"

"Henry Connolly . . . ?"

"Yes. Otherwise known as: *your* grandpa. And I

know you very well. And something's wrong. What is it? Are you feeling all right? Do I need to call someone? Get your cushion?"

Chrissie smiled. "No. No, I'm fine. It's just . . . I feel a bit . . ."

"Disappointed?"

Now it was Chrissie's turn to frown. "How did you know?"

"It's my fault!" said Grandpa, tutting.

"What are you talking about?"

"It's the *train*, isn't it? I knew it."

"You knew what?"

"I knew that I shouldn't have filled your head with romantic ideas about old trains, with all their steam and coal, and their beautiful interiors, and their . . . their . . ."

"*Biddly-da, biddly-da, biddly-da*?"

"Yes, their *biddly-da, biddly-da, biddly-da*!" said Grandpa, laughing, but with a hint of sadness.

"Modern trains don't make that sound. Because the rails used to be stuck together with funny little metal joints called fishplates. That was what made the noise, when the train's wheels went over them. But now . . ."

"The rail tracks are just welded together."

Grandpa smiled. Of course she already knew.

"Don't worry, Grandpa," said Chrissie. "It's fine. It's a very nice train. And, besides, the important thing is, it's going to get us to London. Where I need to be for my operation . . ."

"Yes," said Grandpa.

"I mean, at the end of the day, it's just a train, isn't it?" she added. "A mode of transport. A way of getting from A to B."

"Yes. Absolutely," said Grandpa.

They looked at each other as they said these words, and both of them could see they were doing that thing that people do when they're trying to convince themselves of something they know isn't true. Which is to say the thing, very definitely and quite loudly, while completely giving away with their eyes the exact opposite.

Both of them saw that in each other.

But only for a second, because then the train went into a tunnel.

It was a very dark tunnel, made darker by something strange: as they went in, all the LED spotlights went out. For the twenty seconds they were in that tunnel, it was, in fact, completely dark. Chrissie felt like someone had put a blindfold on her. She couldn't see anything; all she could feel was the rushing of the train through the blackness. It seemed to be going faster than before, but maybe that was just because when you can't see, you become more aware – and maybe a bit frightened – of being in a moving object.

Chrissie couldn't see anything, but she could *hear*

something: under the *whoosh* of the train as it passed through the tunnel, the sound of the wheels on the tracks. It was very faint at first.

Biddly-da, biddly-da, biddly-da.

She strained her ears in the dark.

It got louder.

Biddly-da, biddly-da, biddly-da.

Then louder still.

Biddly-da, biddly-da, biddly-da . . .

Then even *louder* than the whooshing of the train . . .

Biddly-da, biddly-da, biddly-da . . .

Then it just started to fill her head, like there was nothing else, no other sound in the world:

BIDDLY-DA, BIDDLY-DA, BIDDLY-DA!!!

CHAPTER 3

Mahogany

Chrissie looked across the table, but it was still too dark to see anything. She was about to scream "Grandpa!" at the top of her voice – not just because she was frightened, but also because the noise was so loud now – but then, just as she opened her mouth, the train emerged, out into the light. And she could see, through the window, that everything was fine – the train was passing fields, and farmhouses, and sheep, and electricity poles, and pylons, just like before.

But then she noticed that although everything outside the window was just the same as before, the window *itself* wasn't quite the same as before.

First, there was a word on it. That word, in fact, was: *First*. In red. On the glass, in the middle of the window, in an old-style font. That was weird. Though not entirely unfamiliar to Chrissie, as she recognised it from . . . well, from her knowledge of trains, and from her model of the *Flying Scotsman*, which had the same word microscopically reproduced on *its* windows. But, obviously, it was weird, the word appearing on *this* window, *now*. And how had she not noticed it before?

Chrissie frowned. She sat back a little, and her view enlarged. As did her confusion: because now she noticed that the window was surrounded not by hard white plastic, but by wood. Lovely, old-looking, polished wood. Chrissie didn't know that much about different types of wood – she didn't know a maple from an oak from a birch, when it came to trees – but she knew that this was mahogany. That made her frown even harder.

"Chrissie?" said Grandpa.

She looked around. And then her frown cleared. Not because what she saw made anything any less weird, but because everything had become so amazing now that there was just no point in frowning.

Grandpa looked the same. But his seat had become purple. In fact, *all* the seats had become purple, a deep, lush purple, made out of, as Chrissie discovered when she ran her hand along the edge of her own: velvet. And these seats were no longer placed around tables in a long carriage.

Instead, she and Grandpa were sitting in a compartment. There weren't even individual seats any more, but two long purple velvet benches, facing each other. At the other side of the compartment was an inner sliding door and windows, through which Chrissie could see a walkway, and the main train windows.

The lights in the compartment were no longer tiny LEDs, but old-fashioned bulbs, hanging over the seats in antique brass fittings. Above each seat there was a mirror, and then, above that, the luggage rack had turned into a long net. And in between all of this, joining it up, was more of that wood: more of that mahogany.

"What's going on?" Grandpa continued.

"I don't know!" said Chrissie. "Have we . . . gone back in time?"

"Er . . ." said Grandpa, gesturing to the window, "I don't think so."

Outside, the train was going through a town. Presently, it was passing a big branch of IKEA. A man could be seen coming out of the main entrance, dragging an enormous, flat-packed piece of furniture, and loading it with difficulty into the boot of a far-too-small, completely modern car.

Chrissie looked around. The family of four were still there, just staring into their screens, not seeming to notice the transformation of their surroundings. And their screens – one iPhone, one Samsung, one laptop, and one kid's phone that Chrissie didn't recognise – were clearly modern.

"Excuse me?" said Chrissie, to the teenage boy now sitting next to her.

"Yeah?"

"Have you noticed something?"

He nodded. "I have."

"Oh . . ."

"The Wi-Fi's dropped out. But it's OK. I can run . . . on 4G."

Chrissie looked at him, deadpan. "Right," she said. "Knock yourself out."

"I will," he said, still without looking up.

She turned back to Grandpa. "Can you help me walk?" she said.

He nodded. "But where are you — where are we — going?" he said.

"To have a look at the rest of the train, of course!" she replied.

CHAPTER 4

Isn't It Marvellous?

Outside on the walkway, there were many other compartments, stretching into the distance. As Grandpa helped Chrissie along, she saw the Japanese businessmen in one, also ignoring what had happened, talking animatedly over their spreadsheets. In another the bald man was still blowing his nose. His wife was still asleep.

"Is it the whole train?" said Grandpa. "The whole train's become an old train? A *steam* train?"

"Is it a steam train?"

Grandpa shook his head. "I don't know, Chrissie. I've seen a lot of things in my life, but never something like this."

"Well . . ." said Chrissie, breathlessly, "it looks like it from the inside."

They passed the buffet car. Only it wasn't a buffet car any more, it was a dining carriage. It had tables laid out with white tablecloths, and silver cutlery, and glasses. On the middle of each table was a menu, printed in a beautiful old font. Chrissie picked one up: the lunch options today included mutton and peas, steak and kidney pie, sausages and mash, and spotted dick. Which Chrissie correctly assumed was a type of pudding.

"How much further can you walk?" said Grandpa, as they went through to the bit between the dining carriage and the next car.

"Not that much further just now," she said. "But

I really want to see if it is a steam train or not . . ."

"Well . . ." said Grandpa. "Maybe you should go back and rest, and then later—"

"The windows," said Chrissie, turning. "The door windows!"

"I beg your pardon?"

"Look where we are, Grandpa!"

He looked out. They were approaching a beautiful viaduct.

"It's the Ledbury Railway Viaduct!"

"The route bends here, to go around Alnmouth."

"Yes . . ."

"That means the train will bend, too," said Chrissie. "So we'll be able to see the rest of it through the window . . . !"

"Oh. Of course!" said Grandpa.

They huddled together at the window, looking out through the glass, emblazoned with the word *LNER*. It was stuck slightly open at the bottom;

the wind from outside blew up, ruffling Chrissie's hair. She could hear *biddly-da*! *biddly-da*! *biddly-da*! louder than before; and also the distant huff and puff and chuff of what certainly *sounded* like a steam engine.

Even with the train curving, though, the angle wasn't quite right, so Chrissie pressed the side of her face against the glass, peering down the length of the train. The window was old, and rattled, and the *biddly-da*! *biddly-da*! *biddly-da*! was a bit louder now, to be honest, than she would have liked. It was all a lot more . . . *rickety* than the modern train had been.

"I can't really see, Grandpa . . . I can't see the front of the train . . ."

But just at that point, she felt the floor beneath her feet turn further.

And it was true.

They were in Carriage J. The carriages curved

forward from there, in the direction of her gaze: K, L, M, N, O, P . . . and then, yes! At the front of the train, a deep green, that endless apple green that once said Britain; the front section.

A locomotive! Its sides branded, like the windows, *LNER*, pulling behind a wagon of coal, and, at its front and top, a black cylinder cutting through the air – a chimney! – puffing out, in rhythmic blasts, what seemed to Chrissie's eyes perfectly rounded clouds of white, smoky steam.

Chrissie watched, enraptured. The sound and the sight were all she had ever wanted to experience.

"It's a steam train, Grandpa!" she said. "We're travelling on a steam train!"

"How marvellous!" he replied.

"Is it the *Flying Scotsman*?" said Chrissie. "I really hope it's the *Flying Scotsman*!"

They both looked out of the window again. But

then, the train moved back to the left, and the front locomotive disappeared out of view.

CHAPTER 5

Points Change

Going slowly back towards their own compartment, they saw that the bald man had stopped blowing his nose and was holding out his hand for a cup of coffee. Karen had appeared, and was pouring the cup for him. Unlike any of the passengers, though, she looked different. She wasn't wearing her red uniform any more, but rather a grey woollen outfit that looked like it came from a much older time. The coffee pot wasn't a modern flask-like one, either, but was all silvery and posh. She looked up and waved as Chrissie glanced up.

"What's happening?" said Chrissie.

Karen raised her finger to her mouth, shushing her. She finished pouring the coffee, and came outside to the walkway, sliding the glass door open, and then shut again behind her.

"We mustn't disturb the customers," Karen said, quietly.

"Sorry?" said Chrissie.

Karen looked from side to side, as if checking whether or not she was being watched. Then she came closer to Chrissie, speaking even more quietly.

"You've noticed . . . the *change* . . ."

"The . . . ?"

Karen raised her eyebrows, and looked around in a circle, meaning, without saying it: *You know: all this* . . .

"Right," said Chrissie. "Yes. We have."

"Just a bit," said Grandpa.

"OK," said Karen. "But most people . . . don't."

"They don't?" said Grandpa.

"No," said Karen. "Particularly adults. People are so wrapped up in their work now, or their phones, or . . ." She glanced back into the compartment. The bald man had finally stopped blowing his nose. He was now examining his coffee suspiciously, as if it might not really be coffee. ". . . themselves, that generally they don't notice *anything* that's happening around them."

She carried on looking into the compartment for a few seconds, with an expression that could best be described as disappointed. Chrissie and Grandpa exchanged glances.

"So . . ." said Chrissie, reclaiming Karen's attention, ". . . this has happened *before*?"

"Oh yes," said Karen. "Not *every* trip. Hasn't happened for ages, in fact. I think it might be . . ." She looked quizzically at Chrissie. "Do you like trains? Old trains?"

"Yes!" said Chrissie.

"Ah. That's it. It only happens when we've got a passenger on who's dreaming about all that. Who wants to be, secretly, not on a 125mph electric bullet between one city and another but on a *proper* train.

Someone who's thinking more about the train than the journey . . ."

"So . . ." said Grandpa, "we haven't gone back in time . . . ?"

Karen laughed. "Back in time?! No! Look, there's Durham North Road!"

Grandpa and Chrissie looked around: six phone shops and a takeaway called *Krispy Fried Chicken*.

"No, no," continued Karen. "We haven't gone back in time. The *train* has. Just the train. Rest of the world stays the same. Oh, and things that come with the train. Like the food. And this uniform."

"It's nice," said Chrissie.

"It's scratchy," said Karen.

"What about the track?" said Chrissie.

"Sorry?"

"Well – modern track isn't made for these kind of wheels . . ."

"Now you're getting a bit technical for me. I think

it probably changes as it goes along . . ."

"How long does it last?" said Grandpa.

"Not very long, normally. That's why we don't mention it. And why we don't alert the passengers. Most of the time it's come and gone before any of . . ." – she gestured with her head back into the compartment; the nose-blowing man was back to blowing his nose, in fact, now he was doing that disgusting thing of blowing it, then examining his handkerchief to check . . . whatever old men are checking for when they're checking . . . that . . . – ". . . *this* lot have looked up. And the management have decided it's best if things stay that way."

She stopped, frowned, and checked her watch (which had been a digital one, but now was silver, and had a big hand, a little hand, and numbers).

"What is it?" asked Chrissie.

"Actually . . . it's already gone on longer this time than I've ever noticed it before. That's odd . . ."

"And a bit worrying," said Grandpa.

"Why?"

"Um . . . that's why I asked how long it normally goes on for. There's a points change in about one mile . . ."

"And?"

"Well, I used to work this route. And it was always a rough section of track back then. I'm just a little worried that things might get a bit bumpy there."

"Never mind that, Grandpa," said Chrissie, "I need to know something." She turned to Karen, her eyes filled with awe and hope. "Could you tell me . . . this train . . . is it the *Flying Scotsman* . . . ?"

Karen opened her mouth to reply. But suddenly she was interrupted by the train shaking. *Really* shaking. Grandpa was thrown one way, and Karen the other. Both of them ended up on the floor. Only Chrissie – who in order to stand in the walkway in the first place had to hold on to the rail that ran under the window – stayed upright.

"Oof!" said Grandpa, getting up and holding his back. "I think I may have overestimated how far away that points change was."

"Grandpa . . ." said Chrissie, looking out of the window. "I think you may have *under*estimated how worried we should be about it, as well . . ."

CHAPTER 6

The Wrong Side of the Tracks

The train was going very fast now, faster than it should. But more importantly Chrissie, with her eagle eye for everything to do with trains, could see it was no longer on the right track.

The bump at the points change had shifted it on to the *opposite* track: the track, in other words, going in the opposite direction. Well. The *track* wasn't going in the opposite direction. But other trains on it would be.

"We're on the wrong side of the tracks!" said Chrissie.

"What, metaphorically?" said Karen. "We're passing through a bad part of town?"

"No! Really! We're on the wrong track!"

"Oh . . . Is that bad?"

"Well," said Grandpa. "Not until a train appears, heading straight towards us. Then it definitely *will* be."

"Oh goodness!" said Karen. "OK! I'll call the driver."

She reached inside her jacket for her phone.

"What . . . hang on . . . *arrggh*!" she said, taking out not a phone, but a pigeon. She held it away from her, terrified. The pigeon flapped its wings, but didn't fly away.

"What's *that* doing there?" she screamed. "And how long has it been in there?!"

"Look!" said Grandpa, pointing to a rolled-up piece of paper around its leg. "It's a carrier pigeon." He reached out and took the pigeon gently in his arms. "It'll have been trained."

"Not to *not* poo inside my jacket, I can tell you that for starters!" said Karen, looking at some very suspicious marks inside the lining.

"We could write a message on the paper and send the pigeon out of the window to fly to the driver!" said Grandpa.

"I don't think so, Grandpa," said Chrissie. "We haven't got time. Besides, I think the train is going too fast for that now!"

Grandpa looked very worried. As did Karen.

The sound of the wheels on the track was getting faster and faster.

Biddlydabiddlydabiddlydabiddlydabiddly dabiddlydabiddlyda!!!!

"What shall we do?" he said.

Chrissie thought for a second. Then she said: "Fetch my wheelchair!"

CHAPTER 7

More Frightening than *Assassin's Creed*

Three minutes later, Chrissie was being pushed by Grandpa and Karen (holding one handle each) as fast as possible through the carriages. They were virtually jogging. Luckily, the walkway past the compartments was free of people and provided a straight path for them to trundle down at speed.

"Where are we going?!" shouted Karen.

"To the front of the train!"

"What are we going to do when we get there?!" yelled Grandpa.

"You'll see!" said Chrissie. Who, as she said it, knew that *she* would see when they got there, as well. Because she didn't really have a plan. She just knew they needed to get to the locomotive.

When they passed the compartment containing the Japanese businessmen, there was a brief moment when one of them looked up, as if about to point out to his colleague that a Paralympic event seemed to be going on outside. But then he just blinked and looked back to his spreadsheet. After all, they were now on page four.

Eventually, Chrissie, Grandpa and Karen reached the footplate separating the last carriage from the coal wagon. It was very loud there: the train on the track and the puff of the steam and the roar of the wind joined together to make it almost impossible to hear anything. *And* the train seemed to be going faster than ever!

"How do we get round the coal wagon?" shouted Grandpa.

"There's a narrow bit of decking around the outside!" Chrissie shouted back. "You'll have to get me out of the wheelchair!"

"It's too dangerous!" said Grandpa. "You can't walk on that!"

"I can!"

"How do you know?"

"Because I know trains like these like the back of my hand!" said Chrissie. "I've watched models like it go round and round my room for years! I know exactly how narrow the deck is and where the handles are to hold on to on the side of the wagon!"

Grandpa looked at her.

"Karen?" he said, wanting to know what she

thought. But Karen had another problem.

The passengers had finally noticed something was not normal. The family of four were no longer stuck to their screens, the Japanese businessmen were no longer studying their spreadsheets, and the nose-blowing man was no longer examining his hanky. Although his wife was not there, so perhaps she had slept through the whole thing. In fact, all of them (apart from the nose-blowing man's wife) had followed Karen and Grandpa and Chrissie down the train.

Now, they were all shouting at Karen at once.

"What *is* going on?"

"*Dō shimashita ka?*"

"It's more frightening than *Assassin's Creed*!"

"I spilt my coffee!"

"I shall be demanding a full refund!"

Grandpa watched Karen raise her arms to begin calming them down. He turned back to Chrissie. Her face, he could see, was determined.

"All right," he said, grimly. "Let's do this."

CHAPTER 8

About as Train-y as it Gets

Gently, Grandpa took Chrissie out of the wheelchair. She held his hand, and stepped off the footplate on to the small deck. With her other hand, she grasped for the first of the handles that she knew lined the coal wagon. Together, facing inwards, they inched along towards the front of the train.

BIDDLYDABIDDLYDAHUFFPUFFHUFF puffHUFFpuffBIDDLYDAHUFFPUFF!!

There was so much wind noise, and so much train noise, that Chrissie could barely think. She took a deep breath and through her terror, she thought: *So, Chrissie, you wanted to experience being on a train – well, this is about as train-y as it gets!*

But she had to concentrate now – her back and hips ached, and her balance felt shaky; she had never had to do anything like this before. At one point, her footing went, and she slipped towards the tracks – but Grandpa reached out a hand and caught her, returning her to the deck.

One . . . two more inches along . . . and they were there! Across another footplate, and into the driver's cab.

In there, one man in a flat cap was stripped to the waist, shovelling coal into the fire that stoked the engine. Another – the driver, who was dressed in a black uniform – was doing his best to steer the train back on to the correct track. He was slamming again and again on the reversing gear.

"Any luck?" shouted the shovelling man, in between shovels.

"No!" shouted the driver. "It won't go back!"

"Hello!" shouted Grandpa.

They turned around.

"Hey!" said the driver. "No passengers allowed in here!"

Then Chrissie appeared.

"OK . . ." continued the driver. "Um . . . look, while I understand . . . we often have children . . . like . . ."

"I'm Chrissie," said Chrissie. "Pleased to meet you. And I'm not here because I've won a competition. I'm here because the train is going in the wrong direction!"

The driver narrowed his eyes at her. "And you think I don't know that?"

"Well, you weren't sure for a bit," said the shovelling man. He looked at Chrissie. "It took him

about five minutes to work it out."

"Shut up," said the driver.

"What can we do?" said Grandpa. "What needs to happen?"

The shovelling man stopped shovelling. He shook his head. "You know what, old-timer? I really don't know. Look at me. I'm wearing a *flat cap*. My chest and back are covered in sweat and soot. But twenty minutes ago I was a trainee train driver. From 2023. I wear designer glasses. I have an iPad. I'm on Twitter: 2,600 followers."

"His posts *are* great," said the driver. "You should see his rude vegetables series. Hilarious."

"Sorry, what point are you making?" said Chrissie.

"I DON'T KNOW HOW TO FIX THIS!" said the shovelling man. "I DON'T KNOW HOW TO WORK A STEAM TRAIN FROM OVER A HUNDRED YEARS AGO! AND NEITHER . . ." He pointed to the driver, ". . . DOES HE!"

At that point he burst into tears.

"Hasn't it happened before?" said Grandpa, quietly.

"Yes," said the driver. "But that time it only lasted a few minutes. And afterwards, when me and him talked about it . . . quietly . . . we thought it was just a mutual hallucination, brought on by too much . . ." he searched for the right word, and then said: "train."

"ALSO NOTHING WENT WRONG THAT TIME!" shouted the crying man (previously the shovelling man). "WE DIDN'T END UP HURTLING DOWN THE TRACK TOWARDS AN ONCOMING TRAIN AND CERTAIN DEATH!!"

Chrissie coughed. They all looked at her.

"Excuse me," she said. "You've tried stopping the train, I assume?"

"Yes. Of course. But the brakes don't seem to be working."

"What about reversing the regulator," she said, "opening the cylinder cocks as far as they can go, and pushing the Johnson bar forward?"

"Hmmm. No, we haven't done that," said the driver.

"Why not?"

"Because we don't know what it means . . ." said the crying man.

"No."

"OK, we could try that," said Chrissie. "Driver, you get the lever, and shovelling man – you don't mind if I call you shovelling man, do you?"

"Chrissie," said Grandpa, quietly. But very seriously.

"What?" She looked over. He was leaning out of the cab, looking forward.

"I don't think we've got time for that."

With some difficulty – she was feeling tired, and her bones were aching – Chrissie went over to him.

And then she saw what he was looking at, and why he was talking quietly and very seriously.

CHAPTER 9

The *Flying Scotsman*

The train coming in their direction was still about a mile away, on the other side of a short tunnel, but it was coming fast. Very fast.

It was not a steam train, either. It was a modern train, electrically powered. Which might explain why it was coming at such a speed.

Chrissie looked at Grandpa.

"Oh no," she said. "Is there time to avoid it?"

Grandpa shook his head.

"If my memory serves me correctly, there is a set of points just before the tunnel. If our wheels engage with that, we could – maybe – swerve just in time. But I don't think these old wheels will be the right gauge for it . . ."

Chrissie nodded. She had learned so much about trains – although this was one time she wished she hadn't – that she knew he was right.

"So Chrissie," Grandpa continued. "There's only one thing left to try."

"What?"

"You remember what Karen said. That this happens when there's someone travelling on the train who's really in love with old trains?"

"Yes."

"That's you. Obviously. But I think the reason it's lasted longer than usual is that you're more in love with old trains than anyone else, ever. More than me, even."

"Right . . ." She looked out. The other train was coming closer. She hoped that Grandpa would get to his point soon. He did sometimes go on a bit without doing that.

"So I think what you need to do is . . . *not* be in love with old trains. At least for a little while."

"Sorry?"

"I know it sounds strange, but you need to think . . . that you've *done* it. You've been on an old train, you've seen it, you've heard it, you've felt how beautiful it is. There's a grown-up word for that: *fulfilled*. That's happened to you. And now you can let it go. Your love of trains. You can love . . . something else."

Chrissie nodded. She understood. She shut her eyes tightly, and tried. She tried to forget about trains, to think that they didn't fill her sky. But it was hard, here, now. In the dark behind her eyelids, she could smell the coal, and feel the steam, and hear

the *biddly-da*
biddly-da
biddly-da so loud.

She opened her eyes. The oncoming train was near enough to see its front windows.

"No good?" said Grandpa.

Chrissie shook her head, apologetically. As apologetically as she could, given the circumstances. Grandpa nodded, and turned to stare ahead, his face sad and accepting of their fate.

But then, suddenly, not so sad and accepting.

"*That* might help," said Grandpa, pointing.

Chrissie looked. Reflected in the window of the approaching train was the front of *their* train. And right on the front of their train, in the iron circle just below the chimney, the words:

ИAMƧTOƆƧ ƆИIY⅃ⅎ

It didn't take long – a split second in fact – for Chrissie to reverse in her mind the reflected words:

FLYING SCOTSMAN

Then she heard Grandpa say: "You were right after all. We are on the *Flying Scotsman*!" And, in that moment, Chrissie knew what *fulfilled* meant.

The modern train was approaching one end of the tunnel; their train the other end. There was no time left.

"What else should I love?" she said.

Grandpa shook his head, and shut his own eyes. "That's up to you," he said.

And into the tunnel both trains went.

CHAPTER 10

That's What I Heard

Mary Connolly looked at her husband with some anxiety.

"I just *know* something's wrong."

"You don't," said Jim (that's her husband). "All you know is the train is late."

"We should *never* have let Henry bring Chrissie down by herself."

Jim turned away from the platform noticeboard, which continued to say that the 11.47 train from

Edinburgh was running at least an hour late, and looked at her. "Whatever else my dad may have done wrong, I'm pretty sure it doesn't include anything that would *delay the train*."

Mary laughed, but still looked nervous. "I know," she said. "It's stupid of me, but I've asked the guard why it's so late and he just said he didn't know."

"Well, he probably doesn't."

"It's been over an hour!"

Jim looked a bit worried now himself. "OK, if it doesn't turn up in the next five minutes, I'll—"

He was interrupted by a loud train whistle. Both of them turned to look. Coming into King's Cross, Platform 7, was a train that said, on its front, **Edinburgh–London**. It was an ordinary-looking, modern, if very late train.

A minute later, they were helping Chrissie out of her carriage and on to the platform.

"You got upgraded to First Class!" said Jim.

"Yes!" said Chrissie.

"I imagine it was a very quiet journey, then!"

Chrissie looked at Grandpa, who looked back, and smiled.

"Yes. Pretty quiet," she said.

Jim got her wheelchair down from the train. Grandpa stood behind her, ready to push. Chrissie sat in it, and they began making their way up the platform, towards the exit.

"But still exciting, though!" said her dad. "Your first time on a train!"

"Yes," said Chrissie. "I liked it very much!" Then she looked up at Mary. "Mum – are you OK?"

They approached the ramp out of the platform. There was a queue to get past the ticket barriers, so they stopped for a second. In front of them, a family of four were all staring at their screens; two Japanese businessmen were discussing business; and a bald man was blowing his nose, while his wife shut her eyes, possibly because she was asleep on her feet, or possibly because that was the best way of getting past being the bald man's wife.

Mary crouched down. "Sorry, Chrissie, I know I'm being a bit quiet. I got a little worried because the train was so late . . ."

"Oh!" said Chrissie. "Well, that was because . . . why was it again, Grandpa?"

"Um . . . wrong kind of snow?"

"Sorry?" said Jim. "It's June."

"It doesn't matter," said Mary. "I don't think it was anything to do with the train. It was just – you know, Chrissie, you've had operations in the past and sometimes they haven't worked, and before we get to the hospital I just wanted to say that if this one doesn't—"

"It doesn't matter!" said Chrissie.

"Sorry?" said Mary.

"Sorry?" said Jim.

Chrissie smiled. "I mean, I hope it does work. That would be great. But if it doesn't – well, I love my life. As it is. Don't I, Grandpa?"

"That's what I heard, Chrissie."

Jim and Mary looked at each other. Chrissie had never really said anything like that before. But before they could even smile at each other about it, they noticed that all the other passengers had gone through the barriers. The queue had disappeared.

The ramp was clear.

"Go for it, Grandpa!" said Chrissie.

And he – joined suddenly by one of the train staff, a woman dressed in red called Karen – grabbed the handles of the wheelchair, and pushed, and ran up the ramp! Chrissie whooped with joy as they went.

"That's good . . ." said Mary, a bit confused.

"Yes, it is . . ." said Jim, also a bit confused. But they were both pleased.

CODA

When the doctors all left Chrissie's room, having told her the operation had gone very well, but maybe she should sleep now, she nodded. Her mum and dad and Grandpa all kissed her and left the room, too. Chrissie was about to go to sleep.

Just before she dropped off, though, she noticed her window was open. She wondered if a nurse should come in and shut it. But the breeze was warm and nice.

Then she shut her eyes, and the breeze felt suddenly greater. So she opened them again. A bird – a pigeon – had come in through the window, and was in the room. It was fluttering over her bed.

Chrissie was about to ring the bell next to her bed for help, when she noticed, on the bird's left leg, a rolled-up bit of paper. The pigeon came down and curled its wings up beside her.

Chrissie took the paper off its leg. She unrolled it. It was fine, cream-coloured notepaper, beautifully embossed with the name *LNER*. On it, someone had typed, using what looked like an old typewriter, the words:

Dear Chrissie. Thank you for saving the Flying Scotsman. Thanks to you, it will continue to ride the East Coast Main Line forever.

There was no name. The paper ran out at that point. Chrissie looked at the pigeon, and smiled.

"Thanks," she said.

The pigeon looked at her, and seemed to nod. Then it opened its wings and flew out of the window.

And, putting the piece of paper safely under her pillow, Chrissie Connolly fell asleep. But she didn't dream about trains.

She didn't need to any more.

THE CHILD WHO HAD NEVER BEEN ON HOLIDAY

Illustrated by Steven Lenton

CHAPTER 1

Every Year. Without Fail.

"Dad? Where are we going?" said Max.

"Don't be an idiot, Max," said Colin without looking round.

Colin was Max's dad. Max was eleven. I'm not sure how old Colin was. He was almost totally bald, and what hair he had, bunched round the sides of his head, was grey. So not a young dad.

"You know where!" he said.

"Where are we going, Mum?" said Lily.

"Don't be stupid, Lily," said Sarah, also without looking round.

Not turning round was a good idea as she was driving. It was a particularly good idea as she was driving on a motorway, and outside it was raining hard. Sarah was Lily's (and Max's) mum. Lily was eight. Sarah never told anyone her age.

"You also know where!" she said.

"WHERE WE GOING, MUMMY AND DADDY?" said Jack.

Jack was Lily and Max's little (four and a half years old) brother. Colin and Sarah were his parents too. Obviously. Not sure why I felt the need to tell you that. I've put his words in capitals as he only really spoke via the medium of shouting.

"Oh, come on!" said Colin. "You've just taught him to say that! Haven't you, Max?"

"Actually, it was Lily," said Max.

"NO IT WASN'T!" said Jack.

"Yes it was," said Lily.

Jack considered this for a second. Then he blinked and cried again: "WHERE WE GOING, MUMMY AND DADDY?"

Colin sighed. Now he did turn round in the passenger seat.

"You know where we're going! All three of you! To my mum and dad's house! In Snoring-on-Sea! That's what we – the Hudson family – do for our summer holidays! EVERY YEAR. WITHOUT FAIL. OK?"

He stared at the children. The rain beat down relentlessly on the car windows. No one said anything. Eventually, Colin turned and faced the front again, just in time to see a sign that said:

CHAPTER 2

Snoring-on-Sea

You might think that Snoring-on-Sea sounded like a dull town. After all, it's called Snoring-on-Sea. Then again, you might think it *can't* be dull as that would be a bit too obvious. Or maybe that it can't be dull because the people who live there, on realising what visitors might think when they see the name, would try as hard as they could to defy expectations and make the place really exciting. You'd be wrong. Or right in the first place. Either way, as far as Max and Lily were concerned, it was very dull. And Jack thought so too – even though he was still young enough to find a sippy cup of weak squash exciting – because Max and Lily were always telling him how dull the town was.

As the Hudson family car went slowly down Snoring High Street, the boringness of Snoringness – sorry, that should just read Snoring – became more obvious. It had some shops, but they were mainly charity ones. There was a café – called Iced Delights – which served tea and coffee in green cups and saucers that looked like they'd been bought in 1962. (Because they had.) Iced Delights did serve ice cream as well, but only vanilla, chocolate and rum 'n' raisin, which they were keen to tell you had no actual rum in it, and indeed, as far as the children could tell, no raisin. There was a supermarket that wasn't very super, and which had had a number of sensible names over the years – Food World, Budget

Mart – but now for some reason was called Plondit. And there was a pub, the Wig and Bucket, which the Hudsons never went into as it was just too depressing, even by Snoring High Street standards.

The car turned right past a statue of some old admiral and on to the coastal road. Obviously, one thing that Snoring-on-Sea did have was sea, which is normally not boring. However, Max and Lily didn't bother to look through the rain-spattered windows at it. They'd seen it many times before. The ocean was grey. Just as the sky and the sand were. It was almost as if someone had decided to match the outside world with their dad's hair.

Facing the sea was a row of small terraced houses that all looked the same. They came to the last house at the end of the drive. Before they had even parked the car, the front door opened, and their grandparents were standing in the porch, waving.

"Hello!" said Grandpa Harry.

"Hello!" said Grandma Harriet.

"Welcome back to Spenny-an-Mor!" they said together, pointing at a little sign hanging on the door-knocker. It showed a small boat on the sea, underneath which were written the words – would you believe –

"They always say that when we arrive . . ." said Max quietly as he took his seatbelt off.

"Don't be rude, Max!" said Sarah.

"Well, they do," said Lily.

"It's the name of the house!" said Colin.

"No it isn't," said Max, opening the car door. "That would be Number Fifty-Four." And then he fixed his face into a smile, and said: "Hello, Grandma and Grandpa!"

CHAPTER 3

The Most Exciting Thing in the World

"We've kept your room just as you like it!" said Grandma Harriet, opening the bedroom door and striding inside.

"Oh," whispered Max to Lily, standing in the doorway. "With the wallpaper with weird spots of brown on it that look like poo? And the window that doesn't shut properly with the view of next-door's wall? And the smell of next-door's cooking? And the beds with beige nylon sheets that we slip out of?

And the one-bar heater that crackles all night like it might explode?"

"Shh . . ." said Lily, although she was smiling.

"What were you saying, Max?" said Grandma.

"It's all good, Grandma," said Lily. "He was just saying how right you are, that you've kept the room just the same!"

"Ah!" said Grandma Harriet, hugging Max very tightly to her chest.

Grandma Harriet always wore some kind of antique all-in-one-bodysuit underwear that the children never wanted to think about. But not thinking about it was very difficult for Max at that moment as his face was squashed up against it. "What a good boy!"

"Ugh," he said.

"And now let's have tea!"

Downstairs, the radio – which was a very old one,

with a massive round dial – was on. It was always on in the background of Grandpa Harry and Grandma Harriet's house. It was also always tuned to the same station – it had a little bit of yellow sticky paper stuck on the dial, which said, with a lot of arrows, **PLEASE NEVER MOVE FROM HERE!** – that played no music, but was just boring people speaking about boring things to do with the news. You couldn't hear most of it anyway because every time anyone turned on what Harry and Harriet called the Big Light, the radio would start crackling and making a high-pitched whining noise.

"So . . . with inflation running so high, the only option for this government is . . ." someone on the radio was saying as tea was served.

Tea, in Grandpa Harry and Grandma Harriet's house, meant dinner (although they had it at teatime, about 5pm). And it was always the same: fish and chips and peas. Who doesn't love fish and chips and peas? Well, Max and Lily and Jack actually, after having it every day for two weeks. Admittedly, this was the first tea of the holiday, so it hadn't got boring yet. But, as Max put the first piece of battered cod in his mouth, he felt he could taste the fact that it was going to be on his plate again and again for thirteen more days. Lunch would be pie and mash, and breakfast a full English with beans and sausages, fried bread, bacon and eggs.

This, you may have spotted, is not a very healthy diet. But there's something I haven't told you: this story takes place in 1978 (which, to be fair, means that the crockery at Iced Delights wasn't *that* old), and people then didn't know about things like health. They'd heard of the word 'health', but they didn't really consider doing anything about it, as regards what they put in their bodies.

There was also a drink that Grandpa Harry called pop. He bought it from Plondit, and it was called Lemony Fizz-a-Lot. It was lemon flavour. "Some pop?" Grandpa would say at various points during the meal. Then, without waiting for a yes or no, he would pour a little bit into Max and Lily and Jack's orange plastic cups, and they would drink it through very curly straws. These straws had started out transparent, but had gone a bit cloudy over the years.

In 1978, a fizzy drink was, for most children, the most exciting thing in the world. This, you have to remember, was a time before FIFA and TikTok. We used to dream about fizzy drinks. I mean, we actually did. My older brother once said in his sleep – I shared a room with him so I heard it – "Can I have some lemonade?"

Grandpa Harry always poured just a tiny amount of Lemony Fizz-a-Lot into each cup. But he always left off the top of the bottle, which meant that by the time the drink got into those cups it had no pop and didn't fizz-even-a-little.

"You love a bit of pop, don't you, kids?"

"I do," said Max. "If only this had a bit."

"Eh?" said Grandpa Harry.

"Shut up, Max, you idiot," said Colin, coming into the room and turning the Big Light on.

"EEEEEEEEEEEE!" went the radio.

"It's going to be a long fortnight," said Lily.

CHAPTER 4

Another Thing People Did in the 1970s

It won't surprise you to know that, apart from eating the same meals over and over again at their grandparents' house, there wasn't much for Max and Lily and Jack to do in Snoring-on-Sea in 1978. In fact, it probably won't surprise you either that the only other thing to do was to go to the seaside.

Which was why the very next day – after eggs, bacon, beans, sausages, and fried bread obviously – Max and Lily and Jack found themselves in Snoring

Bay, using saucepans to make sandcastles.

It was mid-morning. They had arrived an hour earlier with their parents and spent that hour in and around Martin and Norma's caravan. Martin and Norma were friends of Colin and Sarah, and they – you'll know this already – owned a caravan. They kept it in a caravan park just behind Snoring Bay. The caravan was very small, and had a toilet – which was very, very small – that contained a pool of terrifyingly blue water. Martin and Norma and Colin and Sarah sat outside, in a square of fold-up deckchairs, drinking beer, even though it was only mid-morning. This was another thing people did in the 1970s. In fact, sometimes those people included children, but thankfully not these three.

Martin and Colin were wearing swimming trunks – quite tight and rather skimpy swimming trunks. And they both had very bushy hairy chests. Unlike Colin, Martin did seem to have some hair on the top of his head, but this was an illusion created by something that was popular with balding men at the time called a comb-over. Norma and Sarah were in bikinis, the tops and the bottoms of which didn't match. So all the adults were wearing swimming trunks or bikinis even though the sun wasn't shining. In fact, it was drizzling, but this didn't seem to bother them in the slightest. Perhaps because they all had glasses of beer. I'm sorry. This was what things were like in 1978. The only reason I'm not saying they were smoking is because I'm not allowed to.

As well as the grown-ups, there was Martin and Norma's son, Mark, who was seventeen. He wasn't wearing trunks, but very flared jeans and a T-shirt with a picture of some sort of leaf on it. Max and Lily and Jack liked the idea of being friends with a seventeen-year-old, and hoped he might want to play with them, but whenever they suggested football or swimming, for example, he'd just look blank and say, "Yeah, whatever, man," and not join in.

So eventually the children had given up on the caravan park and, as always, had gone to the beach. With saucepans. A long time ago Max and Lily had got bored with the three shapes in the sand they could make with the three buckets that the Hudsons regularly brought with them to Snoring and so had started improvising. They had one round pan – an enormous copper one from Grandpa and Grandma's house, which looked like it should belong in a museum; another that was slightly smaller, and a chip pan that had been used so much it had a deep layer of black grease round the inside that seemed as if it could never be removed.

"THIS DOESN'T WORK!" shouted Jack – in tears – as, for the fourth time, he tried to create the bottom layer of a sandcastle. What actually came out was just a kind of sand crumble. This was partly because half of it had got stuck in the grease. Also the sand at Snoring Bay was always damp, but not in a good way: not in a way that meant it stuck together like cement.

"Oh dear," said Max. "Sorry, Jack."

Max was quite a naughty boy, at least in the way that he spoke to adults, but he was a good and caring brother to his younger siblings.

"I wish there was some way I could make it better. I wish there was some way that we could make a holiday in Snoring-on-Sea exciting and fun for you. It's too late for me and your sister of course – our childhood has already been blighted by it . . ."

"Blighted?" said Lily. "Bit strong!"

"I'm sticking with it," said Max, continuing to look at Jack. "But if we could turn it round for you . . .

somehow . . . that would be –" he looked out to sea – "good." The 'good' didn't sound very hopeful though.

"Shall we go for a swim?" said Lily despondently.

"Well, the tide looks about –" Max screwed up his eyes – "a hundred miles out. I think it might be quicker to walk back home again. And by home I mean our actual home, not our grandparents' house."

"Yes," said Lily. "Plus, when we get in the sea, it will be colder than the coldest thing known to man. It will be colder than ice, which doesn't even make sense as it's liquid."

"It seems to be even further away than normal," said Max, still gazing out to sea. "Look at the Island."

Lily and Max turned to look. The Island wasn't really an island. Or maybe it was. It's hard to know what makes an island an island, as opposed to a rock in the sea. Which is what it looked like most of the time. Most of the time, in fact, it was hard to tell how big it was as the sea covered a lot of it. But Max and Lily and Jack called it the Island. They often saw it from the beach and had given it that name. Now and then they even thought about trying to reach it. Some days it looked more like an island than a bit of rock, and today was one of those days.

Lily screwed up her eyes. "Oh . . ." she said. "We could probably walk to it! Or paddle . . ."

"We could," said Max. "But what if we get there and the tide comes back in again round it . . . ?"

"Well," said Lily, "the sea looks quite a long way away from it at the moment."

"Yes." He looked round. "Should we go back and tell . . . them?"

Lily shrugged. "By the time we do that, it might be too late."

They looked at each other, not sure what to do.

"LET'S GO!" shouted Jack, and ran off towards the Island.

CHAPTER 5

The Island

Even though the Island *was*, as Lily said, a lot closer to them than the sea, it still took them a while to get there. There were loads of puddles and pools in the sand, which they had to splash through, and once Jack's feet got really sandy he kept on stopping and sitting down to brush it off. Eventually, just to hurry things along, Max picked him up and carried him on his shoulders.

Eventually, the three of them arrived at the

Island. It was bigger than they'd thought, big enough that from the front you couldn't see what might be on the other side. It rose from the sand in a group of different rock formations. Luckily, none of them were sharp. The sea had smoothed them out into a series of big round grey discs, all fallen on top of each other. In the middle of the Island though, these had fused together to make what looked like a tiny mountain.

"OK," said Max, putting Jack down, "I guess we're here."

"Yes," said Lily.

"WE DIDN'T BRING THE SAUCEPANS!" said Jack.

"Well, you can't make a sandcastle out of rock, Jack," said Lily.

Max raised his foot and stood on one of the big round grey discs. Then he was joined by Lily, and Jack scrambled up after them.

They stood there for a while, looking back at the beach. Max sighed.

"Well, here we are," he said. "We've seen this island every summer, year after year, and never set foot on it. Now we have. And even that — thank you, Snoring-on-Sea! — has turned out to be dull."

"Max . . ." said Lily, looking at Jack, wanting it to seem exciting for him at least.

"DULL!" said Jack.

"Ha!" said Max. "DULL DULL DULL DULL DULL DULL!"

Jack joined in, and they both said it together.

"DULL DULL DULL DULL DULL DULL!"

Lily shrugged. *If you can't beat 'em, join 'em*, she thought. And then they were all shouting at the tops of their voices, on this deserted island in the middle of this deserted beach:

"DULL DULL DULL DULL DULL DULL D—"

"Hello?" said a voice.

The three children stopped and turned round.

A boy – or it might have been a girl – was standing there.

It wasn't a deserted island after all.

CHAPTER 6

Let's Skim!

"Hello?" said Max.

"Hello?" said the boy – or it might have been a girl. He or she was wearing blue shorts and a white T-shirt. They had long dark hair. They were quite small-framed. Their eyes were very black.

"OK," said Lily, "let's not say hello
again. Well, actually, I will. Hello. I'm Lily."

"Lily," repeated the boy or girl quietly, with a
sense of wonder, as if they'd never heard that name
before. Which was possible.

"I'm Max," said Max.

"Max." They repeated this in the same way.
Which was also possible. (That they'd
never heard that name before.)

"JACK!"

"Jack." Hmm. That name
was also repeated in the
same way. Which
was strange.
(They *must*
have heard *that*
name before.)

There was
a pause.

"Normally," said Lily, "this is where you tell us *your* name."

"Oh!" they said, frowning as if unsure. But then their face cleared.

"Ariel!"

Max stared at the child. "Like the washing powder?"

Ariel looked puzzled. "I don't know."

"Is that a boy's name?" said Lily.

Ariel frowned again. "I . . . guess so?"

"You guess so?"

"It *sounds* like a boy's name," said Ariel. "Kind of."

"SO YOU'RE A BOY?" said Jack.

"Are *you* a boy?" said Ariel.

"I CERTAINLY AM!"

"WELL THEN, SO AM I!" Ariel shouted back. And, for the first time, he smiled.

"Right, well, this is weird," said Max.

"Do you skim?" said Ariel.

"Swim?" said Lily.

"Skim. Come with me."

They followed him to the other side of the Island. It wasn't a long walk. Ariel hopped easily from disc to disc, even though they were wet and slippery. Round the other side of the tiny mountain, the sea was in view. In fact, it was considerably closer to them than when they'd set off from the beach.

"Oh!" said Lily. "The tide's coming in!"

"Yes!" said Ariel. "Which is good skimming news . . ."

"But not so good not-drowning news?" said Max.

Ariel looked at him. He smiled again. "No idea what that means!" he said. "But anyway. Look!"

He bent down. The edge of the Island, where the rocks met the sand, was covered with pebbles. He held one up. It was like the big discs that the Island was made up of, only much, much smaller.

"This is perfect."

"Hold on!" said Max, crouching down. "Hey. You're right. This is a treasure trove for skimming!"

He picked another perfectly disc-shaped pebble.

"Let me have a look!" said Lily.

"AND ME!" said Jack.

They both quickly picked similar ones. All four children now had stones. They held them up.

"Fantastic!" said Ariel. "Let's skim!"

CHAPTER 7

Fly!

M ax looked out. The sea was close now, only about five yards away.

"OK, but quickly! I'll go first! You all watch!"

He ran towards the ocean. There was sand again under his feet, in between the Island and the edge of the water. Max liked to think of himself as pretty good at skimming. He had his own little technique where he waited until the last minute and then flicked his wrist sharply.

As his feet touched a wave, he went for it. *Flick!*
The stone left his hand and . . . *skim! Skim! Skim!*
Three hits on the water. It went quite a long way. He
turned round, pleased with himself.

"Good work!" shouted Lily. "Now my turn!"

Lily was confident. She strode towards the sea and, with less of a flick, more of a throw, her pebble hit the water, and again *skim! Skim! Skim!* It was three

dunks across the surface, ending up more or less in the same place as Max's.

She turned, smiling. Max and Ariel were applauding. She bowed.

"OK, Jack, now you have a go!" she said.

"I DON'T WANT TO!" said Jack. He had tears in his eyes.

Lily came over and crouched down beside him.

"Oh, come on, Jack! It'll be fun!"

"I DON'T WANT TO! I'M ONLY LITTLE! I'LL GET IT WRONG AND YOU'LL ALL LAUGH AT ME."

"That is a possibility," whispered Max.

"I HEARD THAT!"

"OK, well, the tide's coming in," said Lily, "so maybe we should just start to get—"

"It's fine," said Ariel, crouching down too so that his eyes were at the same level as Jack's. "I'll help you."

"You will?" said Jack, finally speaking quietly.

"Yes. Give me your hand."

Jack held it out, and Max and Lily watched, a little uncertain, as Ariel put the stone that he'd been holding into Jack's hand.

"It's lovely, isn't it? So shiny and smooth. So ready to be thrown into the sea . . ."

"Yes," said Jack still quietly.

"So . . ." said Ariel. He took Jack's hand, and they walked towards the water followed by Lily and Max. Once at the ocean's edge, Ariel crouched down again. "What you need to do, Jack, is just . . . imagine it. Imagine that stone flying. Flying across the sea all the way to other lands. Can you do that?"

"Yes . . ."

"Good. So, when I say fly, you let fly. You let the stone go. Yes?"

"Yes . . ." said Jack again.

Slowly, Ariel put his hand over Jack's and drew it back. The others watched, rapt. Then suddenly, with the slightest movement of his wrist, he flicked his hand forward, moving Jack's at the same time, and said: "Fly!"

Jack released the stone. It went about three feet across the water and disappeared under the foam.

"Oh . . ." said Max. "Never mind, Ja—"

And then the stone came back again. It rose up from the sea like a flying fish and seemed to hover above the water, before dropping back towards it. But it didn't just hit the water like a normal skimming stone. It dived down under the waves, and then came up again, up and down, over and over and over again, until finally it disappeared from view somewhere far out to sea.

"Wow . . ." said Lily.

"Wow . . ." said Max.

"Good one, Jack," said Ariel.

"THANK YOU!" said Jack.

"Oh no!" said Lily, looking down at her feet. Water was covering them. "The tide's really coming in fast now! We have to go!"

"Yes," said Max. "Come on, Jack!"

They turned and started to walk towards the other side of the Island. Then Max noticed something and turned back.

"Aren't you coming?"

Ariel was just standing at the edge of the Island, looking at them. His feet were invisible under the sea.

"Where?"

Max frowned. "To wherever you live. You can't stay here!"

"I can't?" said Ariel.

"COME WITH US! COME TO OUR GRANDMA AND GRANDPA'S HOUSE! COME TO SNORING WHERE WE GO FOR OUR HOLIDAYS EVERY YEAR!" shouted Jack. "PLEASE!"

Ariel looked at him. He seemed to be considering something. Then, from afar, from somewhere way out to sea, there came a strange sound, a high-pitched drone, almost electronic.

Max and Lily looked confused, but Ariel seemed to be listening to it. He nodded, as if it was telling him something. Then it stopped just as suddenly as it had begun.

"OK!" he said.

CHAPTER 8

A House on Wheels

"The weather's rubbish, isn't it, Norma?" said Colin.

"It's always rubbish, Colin. Snoring shouldn't bother with a weather forecast. They should just put up a sign that says 'raining'. It's not even interesting rain – never a storm – just drizzle. Every day . . ."

"Hello . . ."

The adults turned round. Jack and Lily and Max were standing there. With them was a small-framed child with dark hair.

"Oh hello, kids!" said Sarah. "Who's this?"

"My name is Ariel."

There was a pause. The adults looked at each other.

"Like the washing powder?" asked Norma.

"I don't know," said Ariel. "But it's very nice to meet you."

"Are you from Snoring?" said Martin.

Ariel thought about this for a moment. "Is the beach in Snoring?"

The adults all looked at one another again.

"It is called Snoring Bay," said Colin, "so, yes." It seemed for a moment as if he was going to add "you idiot", but, seeing as this child wasn't one of his, he managed to restrain himself.

"Well, it's nice to meet you too," said Sarah, leaning back in her deckchair and shielding her eyes, almost as if the sun was coming out. (Which it wasn't.) "So, girls and boys, off you go now and play . . ."

"Do you want to come, Mark?" said Max.

"Yeah, man, definitely," said Mark. He didn't move.

"Um . . ." said Lily, looking at Ariel. "Sorry. This is kind of boring, I guess."

The children had gone inside the caravan and were now sitting squashed up together on the main room's – well, its only room's – tiny sofa.

"What is?" said Ariel. He was standing up, gazing around, his dark eyes wide.

"Er . . . this?"

Ariel looked at her, and at Max and Jack who were nodding.

"No!" he said. "It's *amazing*!"

The other children stared at him.

"I've never seen anything like this!" he said. "A house on wheels!"

"Well, yes," said Max. "I suppose it is that."

"It could go anywhere!" said Ariel.

"Yes . . . It doesn't though. It stays here all year."

This didn't seem to matter to Ariel. "It's a live-in chariot!"

"Kind of," said Max. "Although I believe it's called an Avondale?"

"What is this?" said Ariel, turning round. Lily got up to see what he was pointing at.

"It's a kitchenette."

He looked at her blankly.

"You can cook food in it. But I don't think Martin and Norma do very often. They mainly get chips from the high street."

"And look at that amazing thing you're sitting on . . ."

"The sofa?" said Lily.

"Yes. It's beautiful. I love the way it pushes the three of you together, like you're almost hugging."

"Hmm . . ." said Max. "It's not actually that comfy."

"No," said Lily. "It has the thinnest seat cushions ever."

"Yes!" said Ariel. "It's like it's been sliced super-thin by a great . . . cushion . . . chef!"

He peered out through the (also very thin) window. This involved moving a curtain that looked like it might actually have been a shower curtain. Outside, Sarah and Colin and Martin and Norma were still sitting in their deckchairs.

"And your parents and their friends – they're incredible!"

Max and Lily looked at each other.

"In what way exactly?" asked Max.

"Well," said Ariel, "their clothes!"

Lily laughed. "They're hardly wearing any!"

"Yes!" said Ariel. "It's so funny! Especially the men! Why are they sitting there in swimming trunks, but not going swimming?"

Max grinned. "That's what they do!"

"Why are the swimming trunks so small?"

Lily shook her head. "No one knows."

"Crazy," said Ariel. "Also, they're very hairy. Except on their heads. Although your dad's friend – Martin? – he seems to have taken the hair on one side of his head and grown it very long and then placed it carefully over the top to make it look like he does have lots of hair . . ."

"Yes," said Max. "It's called a comb-over."

Ariel looked out at Martin in wonder. "Amazing . . ." he said.

CHAPTER 9

Iced Delights

"I've never tasted anything like it!" said Ariel.

"Yes, well, that's what I thought the first time I tried the rum 'n' raisin without rum or raisin," said Max.

They were sitting at a green plastic table – one of five – in Iced Delights. The parents seemed to be intent on just sitting outside the caravan all day, so Sarah had forced Colin – she always had to force him to do this – to give them some money for ice

creams. They were allowed to go on their own –
another thing that happened a lot in the 1970s.

Max and Jack and Lily were having chocolate ones,
which was Iced Delight's least unpleasant flavour.

"It's delicious!" said Ariel, taking
another spoonful.

"OK . . ." said Max
doubtfully.

"Ariel," said Lily, "where
are your mum
and dad?"

He licked the spoon. "Away,"
he said. "They go away a lot.
And, even when they're
around, they mainly
just let me
do my own
thing."

Max and

Lily nodded. They were used to that themselves. So was I when I was their age. Parents in the 1970s just let their children go out all the time and hardly bothered to ask where they were going. For parents, having children back then was a bit more like having pets. They just fed them and then forgot about them, apart from having a vague sense that they were around *somewhere*.

"But where do you live?" Lily continued.

Ariel held the spoon in front of his mouth. "Snoring. I thought we'd established that?"

"Yes . . . but *where* exactly?"

He looked at her. "On the Island."

"YOU CALL IT THE ISLAND?" said Jack.

"THAT'S WHAT WE CALL IT!"

"But you *can't* really live there," said Max. "It's not actually an island. It's just a cluster of rocks."

"Oh well," said Ariel, swallowing a spoonful of ice cream, "I spend a lot of time there. In fact, I can't think when I've been anywhere else."

Lily and Max frowned at this. But Jack said: "DOES THAT MEAN YOU'VE NEVER BEEN ON HOLIDAY?"

"Um . . ." said Ariel. "No. Have you?"

Max laughed. "This *is* our holiday!"

"Yes," said Lily. "You live where we go on holiday. But, if you've never been anywhere else, I suppose you *have* never been on holiday. We come here every year."

"Oh! How exciting!" Ariel said, looking out at the drizzly high street. "Hey, what does Plondit mean?"

"No one knows," said Max.

"WE'VE GOT A GRANDMA AND GRANDPA AS WELL AS A MUM AND DAD!" shouted Jack.

"Oh wow," said Ariel. "This gets more fun by the minute. Can I meet them?"

"What a beautiful room . . . !"

"Oh no," Max told Ariel, who was wandering round the bedroom, staring, wide-eyed. "Now you *must* be joking. What about the swirls of poo?"

Ariel looked closer at the wallpaper. He sniffed. "Is that actually poo?"

"Urrgh, no," said Lily. "It's just something Max always says. I wish you wouldn't, Max."

"Ariel," said Max, ignoring her, "I know you're a very . . . *positive* person, but come on." He pointed to the window. "Look at that view!"

Ariel went over to check it out. "It's great!"

"No it's not! It's a brick wall."

"Yes, but if you look at it long enough," he said,

bending towards the glass, "the bricks form a pattern that looks like . . . a dinosaur!"

"REALLY?" said Jack, rushing over.

"Yes," said Ariel, pointing. "Look, it's a stegosaurus!" Jack squinted at the glass. Ariel traced a line with his finger. "There's its legs, and there's its head – and there's its back with all the kite-shaped plates on it . . ."

Max looked over. He sniffed. "Those are just chips in the brick!"

"If you say so, Max . . ." said Ariel. "But what do you think, Jack?"

"I CAN SEE IT! I CAN SEE THE STEGGY-SORE-AZZ!"

"Great!" said Ariel.

"Actually, Max," said Lily, who'd been watching, "I think I can see it too!"

"Right . . ." said Max, trying to sound bored, but finding himself following Ariel's finger as well.

"I've never noticed it before!" said Lily. "But you're right!"

"Ahem," said Max. "That's all very well, but the window doesn't even shut!"

"Yes, that's true," said Ariel. "But if you bend down right here where it doesn't shut, in the gap between the window and the window ledge, you can –" he lowered his head and breathed in slowly through his nose then out again – "smell where the dinosaurs live!"

Jack and Lily and Max looked at one another. Max breathed in a little bit and said: "Isn't that just next-door's dinner? Macaroni cheese if I'm not mistaken . . ."

"But close your eyes . . ."

The children all did so.

"And mix the smell of that macaroni with the smell of the sea that's on the breeze. Now breathe in . . ."

The children all did so.

"And . . . there it is! The prehistoric swamp! So keep breathing in – but open your eyes . . ." continued Ariel. "Now this crack in the glass here. If you look at it closely, you can see . . . it's the wing of a pterodactyl swooping down to attack the stegosaurus!"

"OH!" said Jack. "I CAN SEE IT!"

"ME TOO!" said Lily.

"ME TOO!" said Max. And then looked a bit embarrassed. He felt quite relieved to hear Grandma's voice come from downstairs, saying: "Tea's up!"

CHAPTER 10

Lemony Fizz-a-Lot

"Well, I suppose you think the fish and chips and peas is amazing as well . . ." said Max as Ariel tucked into a plate of food. The children were sitting round the table, as were Grandpa Harry and Grandma Harriet. Sarah and Colin were still out at Martin and Norma's caravan.

"*The oil crisis in the Middle East is worsening,*" came a voice from the radio.

"It's delicious," Ariel said. "But I do live – well,

spend a lot of time – on an island in the sea. So I have eaten a lot of fish." He speared another morsel with his fork. "Although it's not normally encased in this . . ." He seemed to struggle to find the right word.

"Me batter?" said Grandpa Harry. "I make it with beer and powdered egg left over from the war. Do you like it?"

"Love it!"

"Thanking you," said Harry. "Would you like some pop? I know you kids love a bit of pop."

He reached across the table for the bottle of Lemony Fizz-a-Lot, which had been sitting there for a while without its top on.

"Yes, thank you!"

Ariel held out his orange plastic cup, and Grandpa Harry poured a little bit of Lemony Fizz-a-Lot into it.

"OK," whispered Max to Lily, "if Ariel says the Fizz-a-Lot is amazing and delicious, then something's wrong . . ."

Ariel took a sip. He frowned.

"Lovely, innit?" said Grandpa Harry.

"Well . . ." said Ariel. "No."

Everyone stopped and looked at him.

"Rude . . ." said Grandma Harriet.

"Sorry!" said Ariel. "Was it? I didn't mean to be. It's just – I expected it to be *fizzy*. What with it being called Fizz-a-Lot . . . ?"

Grandpa Harry blinked. "It IS fizzy."

"No," said Ariel, taking another sip, "it isn't."

Harry turned to the other children. "Max. Lily. Jack." He held up the bottle. "The Lemony Fizz-a-Lot. Is it fizzy?"

Jack and Lily and Max looked at each other. They'd never said it, but the time had come.

"No," said Max.

"No," said Lily.

"NO!" said Jack.

"I mean, it might have been once," said Lily.

"When the top was put back on it . . ."

Grandpa Harry looked astonished.

"So . . . you've never liked the pop?" he said quietly.

"Hang on!" said Ariel. "I can see this has made everyone feel bad. I am sorry."

"I don't feel *that* bad about it," said Max. "I mean, it's been a long time coming . . ."

"Don't be an idiot, Max," said Lily.

"Sorry, is Dad here?"

"Well, spending a lot of time on an island also means I know a lot about liquid. So I know how to fix this," said Ariel. He took the bottle of

 Lemony Fizz-a-Lot from Grandpa and poured some into everyone's cup. "Now, we have some straws, right?"

"Yes," said Lily. She held up the very curly ones.

"OK. Why have they gone a bit cloudy?"

"I think just over time."

"OK, well, never mind. Everyone take a straw."

All the children did so.

"And you, Grandpa Harry and Grandma Harriet!"

"Um . . . all right then," said Harriet, picking one up.

"I'm not much of a one for straws," said Harry. "What about me false teeth?"

"Oh, they'll be fine, Harry."

He shrugged and took one.

"Right now," said Ariel, "lower your straws into the Fizz-a-Lot."

Everyone did. Jack struggled to keep the straw in his mouth, leaning too far over the table, but he managed it.

"OK . . . good. Now gently, everybody . . . blow."

"Pardon?" said Harry. Although because he now had the straw in his mouth it sounded a bit more like "Pmgho?"

"Blow through the straw . . ."

Heads lowered over their cups, everyone round the table did so. They blew. You could hear the bubbles . . . um . . . gently bubbling inside the liquid.

"I CAN'T BLOW ANY MORE!" shouted Jack.

"Neither can I . . ." said Grandma Harriet.

"All right!" said Ariel.

They all looked up. There was a pause.

"So," said Max disconsolately, "that's it? That's the fix . . . ? Just blowing some bubbles into the Fizz-a-Lot? Bubbles that will just dissolve and leave it as flat as ever."

Ariel smiled. "Drink up!" he said and raised his cup.

Max frowned. He stared into his cup. So did Lily and Jack and the grandparents. You could just about hear a very soft, gentle noise. How to describe that noise? It would be the word *fzzzzzzzzzzzz.*

"Oh!" said Lily. "It's fizzy! The bubbles are still there!"

"FIZZY!" shouted Jack, picking up his cup and draining it.

"How . . . did you *do* that?" said Max.

"I didn't," said Ariel, shrugging. "You did it. We all did."

CHAPTER 11

He Seems a Bit Weird

As usual they finished their tea at 6pm. Ariel looked out of the window and said: "Oh, the sun will be setting soon. I'd better go home."

Grandpa Harry nodded and said: "All right, son. Where do you live?"

"Near the beach!" said Lily quickly. Which was certainly true.

"CAN WE GO WITH ARIEL BACK TO HIS HOME NEAR THE BEACH?" asked Jack.

"Yes, please!" said Max, getting off his chair.

"Don't be an idiot, Max!" said Colin, coming through the door followed by Sarah. "It's getting late."

Max opened his mouth, but then shut it again. He looked sad.

Ariel said: "It's not late, Mr Colin . . ."

"I beg your pardon?" said Colin.

"Well, the sun will be setting soon. But I promise you your children could take me back to my home—"

"Near the beach!" said Lily.

"Near the beach, yes, and still be back before dark."

Colin frowned. "How can you promise that?"

Ariel smiled. "I just did?"

Colin looked momentarily confused. "Yes, I get that you *said* it." He paused. "But how do you *know* they'll be home before dark?"

"Oh, I can see them arriving back here. And it's still just about daytime."

"You can?" said Sarah.

"Where?" said Colin.

"Here. This house."

"No, you –" and it seemed like Colin again struggled for a moment not to say "idiot" – "I mean, where are you seeing that?"

"Oh," said Ariel, closing his eyes, "in my head."

"Right," said Grandpa Harry, looking out of the window. "But it is getting dark." He got up and turned the Big Light on.

"EEEEEEEEEEEE!" went the radio.

"AAARGH!" said Jack.

"What's that?" said Ariel.

"It's the radio!" said Lily loudly, even more loudly than Jack's "AARGH!". "When someone turns on that light, it always makes that terrible noise!"

Ariel listened for a bit.

"That's not a terrible noise," he said. "After all, it's much better than the noise it was making before."

"What noise before?"

"When it was someone just droning on about politics or whatever." The EEEEEEEEEEE! got louder. "It sounds a bit like whales singing . . ."

Lily frowned. "It does?"

"Yes. I've heard it often." And then Ariel pursed his lips and made a sound. It was a strange sound, halfway between a whistle and a hum. It was very high-pitched, but it wasn't painful to listen to. In fact, it was, in a way, beautiful. It melded with the feedback from the radio so that Ariel's voice, harmonising with the electronic noise, produced a kind of song.

A hush fell over the table as they all listened to it.

"That sounds like the noise we heard when we were on the Isl—" began Max.

"Shh . . ." said Lily.

The room seemed held in a kind of spell as they all listened to Ariel's song. Then Colin, who was standing next to the radio, turned it off.

"Oh!" said Ariel.

"Sorry. Thought it was going on a bit."

"You haven't changed the position of the dial, have you, Colin?" said Grandma Harriet.

"No, Mum. Of course not."

"Well, I must go . . ." said Ariel, going through into the hallway.

"Mum? Dad? Can we please go with him?" said Lily.

"YES! PLEASE!" That was actually Max speaking louder than normal because he really did want to go.

"I dunno," said Colin, staring suspiciously at Ariel. "He seems a bit weird."

"Oh, let them go, Colin," said Sarah. "They'll be fine. After all, it is the 1970s."

She didn't actually say this. I'm putting it in because, as I've explained already, although *parents* obviously existed at this point in history, they didn't really do much in the way of *parenting*. And so, although she didn't really say it, this was the actual reason why Sarah was happy to let her children go out quite late with this strange boy.

"All right then," said Colin, shrugging.

See what I mean?

CHAPTER 12

Stand Back!

Back on Snoring Beach, the sun had not yet gone down, but was low enough in the sky to make large sections of the sand turn pink, which at least was a better colour than grey.

"What are these?" said Ariel, suddenly looking down at a spot on the sand.

"Oh!" said Lily. "We left the saucepans behind!"

Ariel laughed. "They're yours?"

"Yes," said Max. "We use them to make sandcastles."

"What a great idea!" said Ariel.

"BUT THEY DON'T WORK!" said Jack.

"I don't think it's *them* that don't work," said Lily. "It's the sand on this beach. It's too wet . . ."

"Oh," said Ariel. "Well, Jack, what you need to do is treat the sand . . ."

"TREAT IT? TO A TOFFEE APPLE?"

"No . . . knead it. Like bread." He knelt and picked up a handful of sand, then pressed it together with his hands, rolling and rubbing it into a ball. Then he put it into a saucepan.

"That one still has some chip fat in it . . ." said Lily.

"That's OK," said Ariel. "It'll help to bind the sand."

"It will?"

"Come on, all of you! Help!"

The three of them knelt and followed Ariel's lead, clumping the sand together. They threw the moulded balls into the saucepans, filling them up to the top.

Then Ariel said: "Right! Turn them over!"

The three of them did as he asked.

"Take the saucepans off!"

And there, sitting proudly on the beach, not crumbling, were three saucepan-shaped sandcastles.

"YES!" shouted Jack.

"Yes indeed!" said Ariel. "But we're not going to stop there. Follow my lead!"

He went into a high-speed flurry, picking up sand, kneading it, and putting it into the saucepans again. Jack and Lily and Max did their best to follow suit. Each time, he – and they, under his direction – added another sandcastle, one on top of another, and another, and another, until eventually, Ariel said: "Right. Done! Stand back!"

"What have we made?" asked Lily.

"I don't know!" said Max.

"Ah, that's because sometimes you have to take a step back," said Ariel. "When you're too close to something, you can't see it for what it truly is."

He moved about ten yards away. The others joined him.

"Oh!"

"Oh!

"OH!"

They saw that they
had made a series of
sandy discs, with a
tall sandy tower in the
middle.

"It's . . . a model of
the Island!" said Lily.
"*Your* island!"

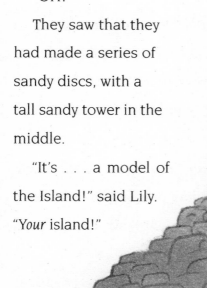

Ariel laughed. "It is. Turns out saucepans are brilliant for sandcastles! Now quickly – let's go to the real one!"

CHAPTER 13

Santa Claws

Jack, Max, Lily and Ariel were again starting on the time-consuming journey to the Island.

"It's amazing how long this takes!" Max was complaining. "How can the sea be so far away?"

"But there is a good thing about that . . ." said Ariel.

"Oh no. Not again!" said Max. But then he added: "Is there?"

"Yes! Look at the pools we're passing!"

"The puddles? They just make it take longer."

"Doesn't matter." Ariel stopped and crouched down. "Taking longer is fine . . . because you can stop and look into the pools to see what's there. Here . . ."

They all crouched down. The sun was still just strong enough to light up the water swirling about in the sand.

"I CAN'T SEE ANYTHING!" said Jack.

Ariel put his hand in the water and shook up the bottom of the pool. As the grains of sand swirled round and then settled down again, a whole series of little crabs appeared, scurrying about and clambering over each other.

"Crabs. Yeah," said Max. "Seen them."

Ariel lifted his hand up. There were ten tiny crabs on the back of it. He stared at them for a moment, then blinked. The three other children blinked at the same time. Then all the little crabs crowded together, and for a moment they seemed to *merge*. That is, they appeared to form just one great big crab: a huge crustacean with an enormous red shell and big inquisitive eyes was now looking up at them, and seemingly . . . smiling.

"Oh!" said Max.

"Oh!" said Lily.

"I CAN SEE A BIG, BIG CRAB!" said Jack.

"Shh, don't scare him . . ." said Ariel softly.

"WHAT'S HIS NAME?"

Ariel looked at the creature. "The Great Old Crab of Snoring Bay," he said.

Jack thought about this for a second. "I PREFER SANTA CLAWS!"

They all laughed.

"Santa Claws it is!" said Ariel.

Then he blinked and the one large crab suddenly became ten tiny crabs again, all scuttling off his hands and back into the pool.

"Come on!" he said and stood up. "No more stopping! Let's get to the Island!"

CHAPTER 14

Not Boring Snoring

When they reached the Island, the sun was nearer the horizon, and the wind was getting up. The waves were rising higher than they had been. Ariel hopped comfortably over the rocks towards the tower at the centre. The other children followed.

"So . . ." he said, turning round, his face red in the light, "Max, Lily and Jack: it's been lovely getting to know you three!"

"DON'T GO!" said Jack.

"Yes . . ." said Lily more softly. "Don't."

"Yes. It would be . . . nice to see you again," said Max.

"Well," said Ariel, "perhaps you will. But now you all need to get home while you still can. The tide's coming in . . ."

"DON'T GO!" said Jack again, his voice starting to wobble.

"Well . . ." said Ariel.

"Before we leave," said Lily, "just explain something to us."

"Yes," said Max. "Who are you? How do you manage to live on this island? Where are your mum and dad? Are you some kind of man-fish?"

"No," said Lily. "That wasn't what I was going to ask. What I was going to say was . . ." She looked at Ariel. "When you first came, it was like –" she waved a hand at the beach and the town – "it was like you were *amazed* at everything in Snoring. Like you'd never seen Snoring – or anywhere – apart from this rock before."

"Yes," said Max. "Which is confusing. That's my point. How can you just have lived *here*? How can you never have drunk Fizz-a-Lot? I mean, on a clear day you can *see* Plondit from here . . ."

"No," said Lily, "that's not my point. My point is: what you did was . . . it was like you were able, just by the way you saw it, to make Snoring-on-Sea – to make our holiday, that we go on every year, to this dull place – seem . . . not boring. Not boring

Snoring. You made it seem – just by looking at it with new eyes – magical!"

"Oh!" said Ariel. "Well, that's good."

"Yes, but then that thing you did with the Fizz-a-Lot – when you made it properly fizzy – and just now, when you made lots of crabs into one crab . . . that really *was* magical. Wasn't it?"

Ariel smiled. "Was it?"

"Oh, don't do that!" said Max.

"What?"

"That mystery 'Ah, who knows?' thing. That's just annoying. Tell us if you're magic or not!"

Ariel laughed. "No, I mean it. When the Fizz-a-Lot went fizzy, I think that *could've* been magic – or it could've been just that we blew some bubbles into the liquid and somehow reignited the fizz that was once there. And as for the Great Old Crab of Snoring Bay . . ."

"SANTA CLAWS!"

"Sorry, Santa Claws . . . one big crab is maybe just what a lot of little crabs hugging each other look like. I'm just showing you that . . . possibility." He turned to Lily. "You can decide . . ."

There was a pause. "OK, that kind of *is* the mystery 'who knows?' answer. But just a bit longer," said Max.

"DON'T GO!" said Jack again.

"I'm not going. You're going. I'm staying. Here," said Ariel. "But . . . thanks to you three, I might not stay here all the time any more because it turns out holidays are really fun!"

"Holidays?" said Lily.

"Yes! That's what I've just had with you three, isn't it? My first-ever holiday. To Snoring. To Iced Delights and Spenny-an-Mor and Martin and Norma's Avondale. I've learned about tiny trunks and comb-overs and shouty dads. I've eaten fish covered in batter from the war and watched a stegosaurus appear from a macaroni-cheese swamp and joined in with the song of an ancient radio." He smiled at the three of them. "What a ride it's been!"

Lily and Max exchanged glances. But then they smiled too.

"DON'T G—" Jack had clearly not accepted Ariel's speech offering the children what grown-ups call closure. He knew that, basically, it still meant goodbye, which he didn't want to say to Ariel. So he felt the best thing to do was just to shout, "DON'T GO!" again. But unfortunately he never got to the O! because a huge wave of water hit him in the face and knocked him over, carrying him out to sea.

CHAPTER 15

What Are We Going to Do?!

"Oh no!" said Lily.

"Oh no!" said Max.

"O . . . K," said Ariel, and waded into the sea. He dived down under the waves at the edge of the Island.

"What are we going to do?!" said Lily.

"I *am* a stupid idiot!" said Max.

But then Ariel reappeared, carrying a very wet Jack above his head.

"WAAAAAAH!"

That was Jack, not Ariel. He carried on crying after Ariel put him down gently on the rocks.

"Yes, well . . . I'm afraid we've been talking for too long."

They all looked around. The Island was now surrounded by seawater. It was an island proper again. And it seemed a very long and watery way back to Snoring Beach.

"Oh dear," said Lily. "Are we going to have to stay on the Island? Like you?"

"I don't think so," said Ariel. "I'm used to it here, but you can't stay overnight. I think you might get very, very cold. And your parents will be very cross and worried."

"Well then," said Max, "when does the tide go back out?"

"In about eight hours."

"Eight hours!"

"Yes."

There was a short silence.

"WHAT ARE WE GOING TO DO?!" Even though I've put this bit in capitals, it wasn't Jack. It was Max.

Suddenly, once again, there was that sound: the long almost electronic note coming from what seemed like a long way out to sea, or perhaps a long way down. Ariel shut his eyes and, like before, nodded. Then he opened them again.

"Skim," he said brightly.

"This is not the time to throw stones in the water!" said Lily.

"Not stones," said Ariel. "Yourselves."

"What are you talking about?" asked Max.

Ariel looked behind him. "I think, with a bit of help from me, you can bounce yourselves along the water back to the beach."

Max and Lily looked at each other.

"OK, either you *are* mad, or magic, or . . ." said Lily.

"You could just trust me?" said Ariel.

She looked around. "I don't think we've got much choice."

CHAPTER 16

Hold Tight!

"Right," said Ariel, "this is what you do . . ."

"You've done it before?" said Max.

"*I've* done it before, yes. I've never taught anyone *else* to do it before." He put his arms out by his sides. "You need to maximise your surface area. Become like a wide smooth stone."

They all followed his advice.

"Great! Now lie down like that."

"Why?" said Max.

"Because you're going to be skimming on your back. You don't want to skim on your front. You'll get too much seawater up your nose!"

"Right . . ." said Max with an air of "that makes sense, but only in a very strange way".

They all lay down with their arms out. Even Jack, who had stopped crying.

"And . . . ?" said Lily.

"Well, that's kind of it."

Lily stood up again. "That's it?"

"Yes. In terms of body position. More difficult is . . . catching the wave. Oh, and of course you must believe."

"Believe what?"

"Believe that you can do it!"

Lily's face fell. "I'm . . . not sure I do."

"Neither am I," said Max, getting up as well.

"WAAAAAH!" said Jack, staying on his back.

"I understand," said Ariel. "But I promise you . . .

all that it took for the Fizz-a-Lot to become fizzy and for the little crabs to become the Great Old Crab of — sorry, Jack, I mean Santa Claws — was for you to *see* it happen in your imagination. So that's all you have to do now as well. You just need to picture yourselves flying on your backs across the sea."

There was a pause. Then Lily was the first. She nodded, shut her eyes, and lay on her back near the water.

Max shrugged. "Well, I suppose it might be fun . . ." And he lay on his back too.

"Wait a minute," he said. "How, from here, do we throw ourselves at the water?"

"Oh, I'll sort that out. You're the stones. I'm the skimmer."

"Pardon . . . ?"

"Waves coming . . . HOLD TIGHT!" said Ariel.

Jack felt two hands on his sides as he was turned

round. And then somehow he was being raised in the air, still on his back, and . . . spun! Spun out to sea! He flew about two feet above the water and then dropped, but didn't sink into the foam. Instead, he glided, hitting the wave – SLAP! – and then again – SLAP! – his back getting wet, but the rest of him staying dry. In his ears, he could hear the rush of the surf and the cry of the seagulls and, in the distance, that high note again. But it didn't sound like a whining droning sound now: more as if someone, or something, was joyfully singing along with each bounce of Jack's body on the water.

After four hits, he grew confident and threw himself up further above the ocean, somersaulting, and twisting, and spinning like a top. Six hits! Seven! It was unbelievable, amazing fun. It was *total* fun.

And then suddenly, with a thump, he was lying

on the sand of Snoring Bay, watching as Lily and Max hit the waves, rising and falling together and then landing themselves, wet but unharmed, next to him near the crab pools.

CHAPTER 17

The Steggy-sore-azz

"OK, children. Time to go home!" Colin was shouting. "Everyone in the car! Now!"

It was a fortnight since they'd arrived. Colin had been packing the car outside Grandpa Harry and Grandma Harriet's house all morning, and was not, as he never was at this point, in a particularly good mood.

"Yes, come on, kids!" shouted Sarah, who was also outside on the pavement.

There was a pause. Silence.

"Where are they?" said Colin.

"I think they're still in their room . . ." said Grandpa Harry, coming out of the front door.

"What?" said Colin. "They're normally desperate to get in the car and go home by now!"

"I'll go and get them," said Sarah.

Fifteen minutes later, Colin was still standing outside next to the family car. He was getting very, very annoyed. In fact, if he hadn't been within earshot of the neighbours, he would by now have been shouting and swearing extremely loudly.

"Right! That's it!" he said to no one in particular. "I'm going in!"

He marched back into his childhood home and up the stairs to what had once been his room.

"Jack! Max! Lily! I am fed up of waiting outside. In fact, I am fed up of putting up with the three of you complaining about this holiday every year and—"

"Shh," said a voice. It was Grandma Harriet.

Colin looked into the bedroom. Inside, Jack, Max and Lily were all crowded round the window. The two grandparents and Sarah were there too.

"I CAN SEE IT! I CAN STILL SEE IT!" Jack shouted.

"See what?" said Colin, still annoyed, but slightly curious now.

"THE STEGGY-SORE-AZZ!" said Jack.

"The steggy-what-now?"

"Shh!" said Grandma Harriet, and because Harriet was, after all, still Colin's mum, he did in fact shush.

"Yes," said Lily. "He's moving through the swamp towards the ocean." She nodded at Max. Max bent down, and Colin saw that they had brought up the ancient radio from downstairs.

Max turned it on.

". . . *Her Majesty the Queen was in Coventry today to open a new bucket factory . . .*"

"Turn the Big Light on, Colin," whispered Sarah.

"What? Why?"

"Just do it!"

He did, and the radio started going, "EEEE EEEEEEEE!" Immediately, Lily joined in with a higher note. "EEEEE . . ." Then Max, a little higher. Then Jack, higher still. Then, most strangely, Grandpa Harry, highest of all.

"What are you do—" started Colin, but then found himself taken aback by the sound they were all making, which did not, as he would have expected, make him want to put his hands over his ears. On the contrary, it was a . . . lovely sound, a strange, beautiful harmony.

"That's a whale . . ." said Sarah softly. "A whale calling from the ocean to the stegosaurus . . ."

The children, still softly singing, looked at the window as if they could indeed see this scene.

Then, out of breath, they stopped. There was a pause.

"Um . . ." said Colin. "We really need to get going."

"Oh," said Lily. "Can we at least stop at Iced Delights and have a rum 'n' raisin?"

"Yes," said Max. "And then go by Martin and Norma's caravan to sit on their very thin sofa cushions for a bit?"

"AND THEN GO AND GET SOME FIZZ-A-LOT! FROM PLONDIT!" said Jack. "AND MAKE IT FIZZY WITH OUR OWN BUBBLES!"

"Well . . . OK," said Colin. "But can we be quick? It's time to leave Snoring!"

"Oh," said Max. "But we love it here now!"

Colin frowned. "You do?"

"Yes!" said Lily.

"Well . . ." said Colin, looking with confusion at his wife, "don't worry. We'll be coming back next year. And the year after that."

"HOORAY!" chorused the three children.

"Now, can we *please* get in the car!"

Max, Lily and Jack looked at each other. Then together they all said, although they knew the answer was home:

"WHERE ARE WE GOING?"

Acknowledgements

I'd like to thank, for all their help in the creation of this book, everyone I work with at HarperCollins, including Nick Lake, Cally Poplak, Tom Bonnick, Matt Kelly, Elorine Grant, Jane Baldock, Sam White, and Tanya Hougham; my illustrators, Jim Field and Steven Lenton; and my agent, Georgia Garrett.

Read the first chapter. . .

PFFT!

CHAPTER 1

★ ORDINARY ★

Billy Smith was ordinary. He was *really* ordinary. For a start, he was called Billy Smith. It couldn't have been a more ordinary name. Unless maybe it was his dad's name, which was *John* Smith.

But Billy, an eleven-year-old boy, wasn't the only ordinary one in his family. Everyone in his family was ordinary. His parents were perfectly nice people with perfectly nice jobs, and Billy loved them, but there was no getting round the ordinary thing. His dad worked in an office. He was a clerk. Billy didn't really know what that meant, but his dad never explained it to him as what it actually involved was just too un-exciting. Too, let's face it, ordinary.

His mum – *Jane* Smith – was a manager at a packing company. Billy wasn't entirely sure what they packed. Some sort of fish. Frozen fish. Or maybe just fish, in general. Once again, she had the good grace to know that talking in depth about her career was not going to set her son's pulse racing. Which was why he remained unsure of the exact temperature or type of fish her company packaged.

Billy's mum wasn't actually working at the moment, though, because she had a baby to look after. Billy's ten-month-old sister, Lisa. You might expect her to be ordinary too. And you'd be right. To be fair, it's quite hard for babies to be out of the ordinary. Babies-wise, in non-ordinary life, there's Jack-Jack in *The Incredibles*, and Boss Baby in *Boss Baby*. Two. That's not very many:

most of the time, even on film and TV, babies just lie around, cry, eat, poo and wee. Which frankly are the *most ordinary* things human beings can do.

Billy was ordinary in every other way too. He wasn't top of his class, or bottom. He wasn't very good at sport, or very bad at it either. He wasn't popular or

unpopular: he had two really good friends, named Bo and Rinor, and went to a very ordinary school called Bracket Wood . . . OK – full disclosure (which may not be that much of a disclosure to anyone who's read any of my previous books). Actually, while Bracket Wood *was* a very ordinary school indeed, some of the pupils were not so ordinary. Or, at least, some not-very-ordinary stuff had happened to them. A lot of magical, or at least semi-magical, things seemed to have gone on in the lives of other pupils. Which, from Billy's point of view, made it worse. Because, although he had heard tell of all these extraordinary experiences (even if he was never sure whether to believe them or not), the school didn't feel at all extraordinary.

Certainly *his* life there didn't. Because nothing like that had ever happened to him.

And then something did happen to Billy Smith. Something extraordinary.

"I wish I had better parents!" Barry said, a third time.
And then suddenly the entire room started to shake…

Barry Bennett hates being called Barry. In fact it's
number 2 on the list of things he blames his parents for,
along with 1) 'being boring' and 3) 'always being tired'.

But there is a world, not far from this one, where
parents don't just *have* children… In this world,
children are allowed to *choose* their parents.

For Barry, this seems like a dream come true, only
things turn out to be not quite that simple…

Fred and Ellie are twins. But not identical (because
that's impossible for a boy and a girl). They do like
all the same things, though. Especially video games.
Which they are very good at. They aren't *that* good,
however, at much else – like, for example, football, or
dealing with the school bullies.

Then they meet the Mystery man, who sends them a
video game controller, which doesn't look like any other
controller they've ever seen. And it doesn't control any
of their usual games. When the twins find out what it
does control though, it seems like the answer to all their
problems. At least it *seems* like that…